Dominic

Lyric of
Dragon Claw Keep

Flapjack Press
www.flapjackpress.co.uk

First published in 2009 by Flapjack Press
www.flapjackpress.co.uk

Printed in Great Britain by www.direct-pod.com

ISBN-13: 978-0-9555092-1-6

This book is dedicated with much love to Rod,
for all his support, encouragement and patience!

Lyric of Dragon Claw Keep

YESTERDAY, ADRIENNE SENT YOU A TEXT.
"I'm coming back. I'll need your help."

Ravaged by rain, you sprinted through the market. Soaked to the skin, you hurtled past shops and banks, nearly knocked over a trench-coated old woman rattling a charity tin outside the chippy. Out of breath but right on time you raced across the grimy station, zig-zagged between dreary commuters tutting and fussing and ran towards platform fourteen. There, nervously shaking the wet from your arms, ignoring everything but the tracks before you, you stood on the platform edge and waited.

And waited.

Adrienne's train arrived an hour late. She stepped calmly from her carriage, black hair shining, black, ankle-length coat rejecting artificial striplights, ready for the weather. She walked towards you, wrapped in rain. For Adrienne, rain was like a loving cat, its body entwined around hers. You couldn't help but smile and pity the fumbling businessmen shaking their oversized umbrellas dry.

You walked together, storm water bounding excitedly about you, back to her place. You showered together and spent the rest of the day in bed.

"Can you believe it?" she whispered, "Just one more day to go. Tomorrow night it will be time."

Rain tapped its jealous paws against the window as you tugged up the duvet, nestled beneath, holding Adrienne tight.

Tonight, it is still raining.

Your head is swimming. Empty beer cans lie by your feet. You can't remember where Adrienne has gone. Stretching out on the settee you crush some papers, the results of Adrienne and you trying to guess the lyrics to 'Love Shack' earlier. "In you, lusty!" scribbled down then scribbled out again.

Kyla yawns. She picks up her beer can from the top of the TV. Brushing purple-dyed hair from glitter-framed eyes, she takes big, clumsy steps over mounds of unlit candles and dolls, piled up between the telly and you.

You look away from Kyla, away from walls smothered in postcards, photos and Blu-tacked pages torn from comics. You look at your hands. Before you left the flat Kyla did your nails purple. Not the whole nail, just a line down the middle of each finger. "Like claws," she had said.

Now, back from the night club, she drops down onto the sofa beside you and smiles.

"I would have killed for just one night like tonight when I was back home," she sighs, resting her hand on yours. "God, if they had a Rock World there, even just for December... Don't let me go back this Christmas. I just want to be round people who actually talk to each other! My family can do without me, right?" Her head lolls to one side and your noses touch. "Make me stay here."

You smile, raise a hand to her cheek. Slowly, your mouth presses against hers.

You kiss.

Kicking some dolls out of her way, Adrienne returns from the kitchen with three mugs of tea. She slams them down on the telly.

"God, Kyla," Adrienne snorts. "You're so needy when you're pissed. Get these candles lit."

Obediently, Kyla breaks out of your embrace, gathers up the candles then pulls the coffee table to the centre of the room. She brushes your wet jackets off onto the floor.

"Can't we do this tomorrow?" Kyla complains, though still setting out the candles in a wide circle as Adrienne had instructed. "I've hardly seen you since you got back. You two had all the fun yesterday whilst I was stacking tins of beans. C'mon," she grins, "let's go to bed."

At this, Adrienne softens, goes over to Kyla and strokes the back of her neck. You stand, hopefully, as Kyla presses her head to Adrienne's chest.

"Don't stress, my love," Adrienne soothes, kissing the top of Kyla's head. "It's Samhain eve, Kyla. The veils are thinnest tonight. This is it." She looks over to you. "Isn't it?"

Quickly, you nod and take your place kneeling by the table.

"I don't want to," Kyla sulks, reluctantly kneeling beside you and joining in the lighting of the candles. "You go reading all this stuff about witches and the dead and think we'll both just go along, do whatever you say. I've got to be up in four hours. I know you don't want to hear this, but... some of us have to work. Isn't it time to..."

Adrienne stares at Kyla. Her voice peters out.

"Clear your mind of thoughts," Adrienne instructs. "I've not spent a year preparing for this just to have you freak out at the last moment. Imagine it, actually being able to speak with our ancestors! It's real, Kyla. Get it together." She turns to you. "We're wasting time."

Putting your right hand into her grip and your left into Kyla's, you watch the flames shiver and dance. Adrienne starts to chant, her eyes screwed up tight.

The ritual has begun.

"Right the Sword. Rise the Flame," Adrienne's command fills the dim lit room like thunder. "Left the Womb. Down the Silent Earth." She opens her eyes just long enough to see that yours are open too. "Shut 'em!" she barks. Immediately you do.

You lose track of how long Adrienne's ritual goes on for, though at no point do any of you hear from your deceased ancestors as Adrienne had promised.

In the blackness between your eyes and their lids, dots of light flicker, prints left by the candles' beckoning flare. Adrienne shouts strange ancient words, and you're aching to take one more look, to watch her at the height of her passion and beauty.

You don't remember when you and Kyla first agreed to this. Adrienne so often speaks of fantastical concepts so wonderfully impossible, and yet never has she been so inspired by any type of magic or witchcraft in the way she has been in her preparations for tonight. So you don't disobey, you focus on the darkness, sit and wait, until Adrienne's final words have entered the room.

There is no sound. You clench your fingers, feel Kyla's and Adrienne's fingers clench back.

There is no sound.

The rain has gone.

"Filth!"

You open your eyes. The table has vanished. So have the candles.

The three of you are still kneeling, still sitting in a triangle, but instead of carpet, rough pebbles and rock lie beneath your knees. Looking around there is no telly, no walls, the whole flat has gone!

Instead, you find yourselves in a low ceilinged cavern, its walls built from large red boulders, its dull light emitted from small, black metal lanterns hung about the cave's roof. In one corner are three steel trunks. Three large wooden framed doorways are set into the red rock face around you.

In front of one of them is a tall, slim, blue-skinned woman, dressed in tight fitting silver armour. She stands above a bleating, cowering creature, a young man with what looks like goat's horns curling either side of his head. Neither of them have seen you yet.

"Wh... wh..." Adrienne tries, but is unable to speak. Kyla's mouth is open and she is staring wide-eyed at the cringing goat boy, just a few feet to her side. None of you let go of the other's hands.

"Filth!" The woman strikes the goat boy across the head with a large, **golden lance**. He cries out in agony as the blow connects. "It is not fitting for a Queen elf to dirty herself dealing with a maggot like you. See what you make me do? Filth!" She raises the **golden lance** above her head.

Frozen with fear, you realise: You are about to witness a murder.

Prepare to Defend Yourself in the Queen Elf's Dungeon!

Somehow you have been transported into these mysterious dungeons, about to witness the Queen elf take on a poor, quivering goat boy. From here on your journey will be a test of survival, a quest to discover why it was you were brought here and, most importantly, how you are going to return home.

Before Battle Begins

To start your adventure you need only turn to panel **1** and from there on make the choices you think will lead to a safe passage home. However, you have a much stronger chance of survival if you first read the advice and guidance offered below.

Use What You Can

In this adventure, you can carry up to six items (such as weapons, wands and shields) at once. If you find an item you wish to take but are already at your a maximum limit, you have to choose to discard an item in order to collect it. If you have companions with you, for example, Adrienne and Kyla, they will usually also be able to carry six items each (unless you are told otherwise). You should note who carries what, as, in battle, items are **not** interchangeable. For example, if Kyla was carrying a **blue shield**, only she would be able to use it to defend herself, she couldn't give it to, or use it to help, other characters.

Entering Combat!

When the word **Fight!** appears, it means you have entered a combat situation and will be unable to leave until the conflict has somehow been resolved. On the left of the page there will be a list. It begins with a description of each of your enemies, including any items they may be armed with. Normally that is all that will be in this list. The exception is if a new comrade has joined your side. Any new comrades who were not with you previously will be at the end of this list, so that you can see what items they have to offer in the fight. Here's an example of the start of a battle scenario:

✒ Fight!

Bellowing Goblin   (Weapons: **icy stick / blue shield**)
Quiet Goblin   (Weapons: **purple stick / blue shield**)

Each character, friend or foe, will take their turn to make a move. Sometimes, when it is the turn of you and your allies, you will be given the choice of which of your crowd to move first. Other times, you will have to advance in a certain given order. When every character has made a move, any characters who have not been beaten will make their next move until one side has won. Some characters who are particularly strong may move more than once in a round!

Attacking

Often, when it comes to your move in a battle, your only option will be attack. If, amongst any items you have found, you have a weapon, you will normally use that whenever attacking. If you have found several weapons, you may be given a choice of which to use, though normally you will automatically use the strongest. If you have no weapon, you attack with your fists. If there is more than one enemy you can choose which you want to attack first. Sometimes one enemy in a group may move out of range, making them temporarily unable to be hit. How to utilise other potential options for your move in battle will be revealed as the story progresses.

States of Health

Every character has three stages of health. Battles normally continue until either you or all your enemies are 'exhausted'.

Fine: All characters begin with no injuries and at full strength.

Bleeding: A hit upon a character will wound them. If one of your party gets wounded and is bleeding, they will remain in a wounded state for all following battles until a way is found to heal them.

Exhausted: If a bleeding character is hit again then they will collapse. If an attack is particularly strong (or the victim's defence is particularly low) a character who is 'fine' can straight away be taken to 'exhausted'. An exhausted character is finished and can fight no longer.

Final Advice

* Your companions will all have their own different strengths and weaknesses. Plan each battle with these in mind.
* Be mindful if one of your party is wounded and starts bleeding. This is a serious state and they are at great risk.
* Do not succumb to the Queen elf's evil ways! Don't cheat or lie. Stay courageous and just.

Now you are ready to begin!

You are in the dungeon, Adrienne and Kyla at your side, watching the Queen elf stand over the goat boy with her **golden lance** raised. She is ready to strike!

Go to 1

1

✍ Fight!

Queen Elf (Weapons: **golden lance / golden shield**)
Goat Boy (Weapons: **metal club / blue shield**)

Queen Elf attacks Goat Boy.
Crack! A successful hit.
The **blue shield** cracks and snaps in two. Goat Boy can no longer use the **blue shield**.
Goat Boy is bleeding.
Goat Boy attacks Queen Elf.
Queen Elf successfully defends herself with the **golden shield**.
Queen Elf is unaffected.
Queen Elf attacks Goat Boy.
Crack! A successful hit.
Goat Boy collapses, exhausted.
Go to 387

2

You walk into a dull, grey hall with an arched ceiling. It is empty. Another small door is in the north wall.

"I can sense magic," muses Kyla. "I think a portal was destroyed here recently."

If you leave by the north door, go to 476
If you leave by the south door, go to 447

3

"I'm not giving up," Kyla declares, pressing her hand hard on the wound she suffered during the fight. "We've got to be brave. We've got to save Adrienne!"

There are three wooden framed doorways set into the rock face around you. In the corner of this red rock cavern are three large steel trunks. Kyla is already lifting the lid of the one nearest you.

"Careful, Kyla!" you warn. "You don't know what's in there!"

"No, it's empty. Oh, wait, there is something, look. A **compass**." She hands the **compass** to you. "If we're going to be searching for Ember we'll need a way to keep from getting lost."

*Make a note that you now have a **compass**. You are able to carry a total of no more than six items at any one time. Kyla can also carry up to six items. Make a note of any further items you collect on your journey, though bare in mind each person with you can carry no more than six at once. Weapons or shields equipped count as items.*

You examine the **compass** and look back at the three possible exits.

If you now look inside the second steel trunk, go to 380
If you look inside the third steel trunk, go to 402
If you leave the red rock cavern through the west door, go to 315
If you leave the red rock cavern through the north door, go to 15
If you leave the red rock cavern through the east door, go to 482

4

Sai howls and lashes out with beak hands.

Crack! A successful hit.

The **blue shield** cracks and snaps in two. Dribbling Goblin can no longer use the **blue shield**.

Dribbling Goblin is bleeding.

Muttering Goblin raises the **purple stick** and casts a '**DEEP HEAL**' spell on Dribbling Goblin.

Dribbling Goblin is fine.

You move next.
If you attack Dribbling Goblin, go to 285
If you attack Muttering Goblin, go to 118

5

Nothing happens.

If you turn the dial left, go to 499
If you turn the dial right, go to 456
If you do not turn the dial again, go to 246

6

Smash! An outstanding hit.

You are bleeding.

Handsome Elf beats his chest and hollers for help.

Warty Goblin comes to his aid!

Go to 508

7

Adrienne attacks Lyric.

Lyric successfully defends herself with the **golden shield**.

Lyric is unaffected.

Go to 403

8

Skinny Goblin raises the **purple stick** and casts a **'DEEP HEAL'** spell on you.

You are fine.

Skinny Goblin raises the **purple stick** and casts a **'DEEP HEAL'** spell on Sai.

Sai is fine.

Go to 374

9

 Fight!

Brigadier Elf   (Weapons: **metal club / golden shield**)

Brigadier Elf attacks you.

If you have a purple glow, go to 400

If you do not have a purple glow, but you have a blue shield, go to 155

If you have neither of these items, go to 143

10

You are just about to step through the north door and leave the gallery when a woman's voice speaks from behind you, making both you and Kyla jump.

"Hours of suffering, my foot!"

You spin round, but no one is there. You and Kyla exchange a worried glance.

If you escape from the mysterious voice through the north door, go to 450

If you shout out to the empty room to ask who is speaking, go to 141

11

"Hello? Um, this is Kyla, and your name is..."

"Quiet!" moans the bubble. "You stupid cretin. Can't you see I'm about to burst? Don't be such a dimwit, bring that **wooden bucket** over here, idiot. Now!"

If you fetch the wooden bucket, go to 44

If you pop the bubble, go to 290

If you leave the bubble to it and return through the south portal, go to 47

12

"Hey, what are you doing?" panics Kyla as you link your fingers into the wall.

"It's OK," you assure her. As the wall's fingers clench yours, toothless mouths exhale excitedly.

"Let go!" Kyla bangs her fist upon the fleshy wall, which wobbles like jelly in response.

"The wall..." You try to pull back your hand. "Kyla, it's sucking in my hand!"

Sure enough, you are already wrist deep inside the fleshy trap. The toothless mouth begins to cackle as you try fruitlessly to pull yourself free, but the more you struggle, the quicker your arm is sucked in.

"Let go! Let go!" wails Kyla, tears streaming down her cheeks. "What's happening? Let go!"

Now shoulder deep, you realise you have lost all feeling in your submerged arm. The hole begins to stretch wider as it starts to embrace your head.

If you have a purple glow, go to 330
Otherwise, go to 194

13

The trunk contains a **blue shield**.

Either you or Kyla can take this item. Whoever takes it will have extra defence if attacked. Remember, each of you can only carry a maximum of six items at a time

If you open the trunk on the right, go to 26
If you leave by the north door, go to 489
If you go back and leave through the east door, go to 431

14

You attack Mollusc Head.

You miss!

Mollusc Head is unaffected.

Mollusc Head roars and vomits projectile acid.

Smash! An outstanding hit.

You collapse, exhausted.

Go to 407

15

Stepping through the north door, you and Kyla find yourself in a very light room, the same width as the rock cavern you just left but about twice as tall. The light shines down through a giant stained glass window high up in this room's north wall. There's no mistaking the image portrayed in the multi-coloured glass; amid a utopian blossoming garden is a portrait of the Queen elf.

The rest of the room is filled, literally floor to ceiling, with various sized golden frames, no more than an inch of pale yellow wall visible between each one. There are dozens, perhaps hundreds, of varying sizes of frame, and in each is a very sketchy painting of a body part. An ear is is one, a toe in another, several of the smaller frames contain nothing more than one brush stroke, which you assume represents a single hair. You guess all the paintings together represent a whole person.

There's one door out other than the one you came in through, a dark oak door in the north wall. On one side of this door is an oak desk with a glass cabinet on it. At the foot of the desk, lying on the floor, is a plaque with some things attached to it. On the other side of the door stands a white bearded man in red robes. He hasn't noticed you yet as he's mesmorised by the paintings around him.

Go to 17

16

  Clawed Dragon swoops!

  Clawed Dragon spews a ball of fire at Kyla.

If Kyla is equipped with a blue shield, go to 416

If Kyla is not equipped with a blue shield, go to 200

17

If you attack the white bearded man, go to 119

If you risk speaking to the white bearded man, go to 308

If you look at the glass cabinet, go to 151

If you look at the plaque, go to 91

If you leave by the north door, go to 450

If you leave by the south door, through which you came, go to 237

18

✒ Fight!

Sketched Lips   (Weapons: none)

Sketched Lips shriek with rage and cast a '**DEEP BOLT**' spell on you.

Bang! A stunning hit.

You are bleeding.

If you want Kyla to move first, go to 131

If you want to move first, go to 117

19

Behind the barred window sits a young goat girl.

"Hey there!" she greets. "If you have any **gold coins**, I'll gladly make an exchange!"

golden lance	**6 gold coins**
golden shield	**6 gold coins**

You don't have any **gold coins**. *You can't buy anything yet!*

"Nice to do business with you," she smiles. "See you again."

If you have a wooden bucket and wish to use it, go to 304

If you leave by the north door, go to 193

If you leave by the east door, go to 450

If you leave by the portal in the south wall, go to 293

20

You take over the jar and rub the paste upon the broken painted lady's lips.

"Wh- what?" A pink tongue darts from the drawing and licks a small bit of the mixture you're applying. "It... it burns! Ugh, no! That's not the right one! What have you done to me? Help!"

"What have you done?" snaps Kyla. "Look, she's in agony! Come on, we should go."

If you hurry out the north door, go to 450

If you escape through the south door, go to 431

If you try slapping one of the other pastes on the broken painted lady, go to 58

21

There is a minute, almost unnoticeable, spark of light. You and Kyla both rub your eyes. You appear to be staring at... yourselves?

Looking at your own bodies, you realise the **'DEEP MIRAGE'** spell has given you both the outward look of your foes whilst making two of the goblins look just like you!

The drooling goblin, the one life left still in his true appearance, is momentarily stunned as it appears his adversaries have quickly changed places. Confused, he lashes out as what he thinks is Kyla.

Go to 76

22

You attack Half-digested Goblin.

Crack! A successful hit.

Half-digested Goblin collapses, exhausted.

Half-digested Goblin drops **2 glittered pebbles**.

You can hold up to **20 glittered pebbles** *and together they will still count as only one item. If you want to keep them, note you have gained* **2 glittered pebbles**.

Go to 185

23

Sketched Lips shriek with rage and cast a **'DEEP BOLT'** spell on Wheezing Goblin.

Bang! A stunning hit.

Wheezing Goblin collapses, exhausted.

Sketched Lips shriek with rage and cast a **'DEEP BOLT'** spell on Lumbering Goblin.

Bang! A stunning hit.

Lumbering Goblin collapses, exhausted.

Go to 25

24

"That **wet sock** isn't purple," you state. "It's red."

"Bah! Know-it-all," **knitted puppet** snarls. "So you're not colour blind. Bet your father is!"

"Is your father colour blind?" asks Kyla. "Is that where this weird hatred comes from?"

"You know nothing about my father!" is the snappy reply. "You want my help or not? Look, if you're an enemy of Lyric's I guess that's good enough for me. Stay away from the tower, for now at least, 'cos that's where she'll be. Arm yourself first. Head north, but don't pull the red lever. Go see my mate Fairy. You'll need to barter with her. I've got something in my hand she won't be able to resist. Get yourself weapons, but get yourself knowledge too, there's no greater strength than being clued up on what you're facing and how to face it. You'll find Ember in the sewer level. Then you'll be sorted."

Thanking **knitted puppet,** you turn away from the cauldron and look toward to the north door.

Go to 199

25

"Wow!" gasps Kyla. "That was... amazing! Where did you learn magic like that?"

"Stop it, you'll make me blush!" giggles the broken painted lady. "You think that spell's impressive, you go see what Ember's got. Keep north. You'll find him, I'm sure of it. Just keep strong!"

Bidding your new friend goodbye, you finally make your way out of the gallery.

If you leave by the north door, go to 450
If you leave by the south door, go to 431

26

The trunk contains several items. One is a bar of **soap**. Another is a tiny **lucky charm**. The last item is a small velvet pouch containing **6 glittered pebbles**.

The pouch can carry more **glittered pebbles** *should you find and want to keep them - this pouch can hold up to* **20 glittered pebbles** *and they will still count as only one item. Either you or Kyla can take any or all of these items if you decide any of them are worth taking. Remember, each of you can only carry a maximum of six items at a time.*

If you leave by the north door, go to 489

If you go back and leave through the east door, go to 431

27

Kyla attacks Wheezing Goblin.

Kyla misses!

Wheezing Goblin is unaffected.

Wheezing Goblin attacks Kyla.

Crack! A successful hit.

Kyla collapses, exhausted.

Lumbering Goblin rushes forward.

Lumbering Goblin attacks you.

Crack! A successful hit.

You are bleeding.

Go to 181

28

"That's so kind, thank you!" she beams. "Look, here."

To your left, one of the frames, containing a sketch of a single finger, begins to shudder and shake. The picture inside splits down the middle, and the two halves part to reveal a secret compartment.

"When I talk, I wear my lips down," broken painted lady explains. "As that artist fool hasn't bothered, I need you to repaint them for me. There is a jar of crushed petals made into a thick paste in that compartment. Put a thin layer of petal paste on my lips and I won't lose my voice."

"There are three jars in here," calls over Kyla, already at the compartment. "They're not labelled. Which one is it?"

"Oh," the smile on the lips drops. "Stupid artist! I don't know. We'll have to leave it. Damn!"

You join Kyla's side and inspect the three jars. Each contains a different coloured paste.

If you want to guess which jar is the right one, go to 350
If you don't want to guess, go to 97

29

You brandish the **purple glow** and wrap Mollusc Head in a distorted aura.

Crack! A successful hit.

Mollusc Head bursts in a slimy shower!

You are coated in thick goo.

Mollusc Head collapses, exhausted.

Go to 249

30

"Not good? Not good?! Everyone's a critic! Oh, my Queen will punish me so when she sees the calamity I have created. I will fetch a ladder to remove these monstrosities and smash each one into pieces before anyone else is subjected to this insult to art. This time, I will beg my Queen to spare a few precious moments for me to study her before I start painting. Please, if you see her before me, will you tell her I am ready for her close up?"

The white bearded man reaches into his robe and pulls out a **lucky charm**.

"I commend you for your honesty. Please, take this small token of thanks to guide you on your way."

If you want to keep it, note you've gained a **lucky charm** *on your items list.*

Go to 97

31

The trunk contains several items. One is a bar of **soap**. Another is a tiny **lucky charm**. The last item is a small velvet pouch containing **6 glittered pebbles**.

The pouch can carry more **glittered pebbles** *should you find and want to keep them - this pouch can hold up to* **20 glittered pebbles** *and they will still count as only one item. Either you or Kyla can take any or all of these items if you decide any of them are worth taking. Remember, each of you can only carry a maximum of six items at a time.*

If you open the trunk on the left, go to 423
If you leave by the north door, go to 489
If you go back and leave through the east door, go to 431

32

As fast as you can, you grab the jar and scoop out a big handful of the sticky paste inside. With far less precision than last time, you throw the paste onto the painted lips. *Splat!* The gooey mess dribbles down the picture and drips off the edge of the golden frame.

Go to 472

33

"Utter tosh!" splutters a low shelf head with a monocle in one eye.

"You don't play cards, do you?" sighs black beard. "Never mind. Oh, and I'm not Ember, no."

"Can you direct us to him?" asks Kyla hopefully.

"Ember went into hiding after he dared refuse to side with Lyric in her war," first head replies. "Go to the sewers, but watch for Dream Molluscs."

"These dungeons are riddled with traps," warns a freckled boy's head. "Watch out!"

If you make your way toward the north door, go to 426

If you go back through the east door, go to 237

34

Kyla breaks down in tears as the broken painted lady prepares the spell to end both your lives.

"We were only trying to help," she weeps. "Please, don't do this!"

The sketched lips open.

Go to 194

35

Attached to the plaque are two **golden lances,** lay one over the other forming a cross. Beneath them, two **blue shields** have been stuck, forming a sort of coat of arms.

If you have a chisel, go to 37

If you don't have a chisel, do you leave by the north door, go to 450

or leave by the south door, go to 431

36

You and Kyla make your way from the glass cabinet toward the north door.

"What a weird gallery," muses Kyla. "I'll be glad to - *eek!*"

The north door suddenly slams back. From the archway a thin, squat, scaly goblin emerges. Wheezing and scratching an open boil on the end of a carrot shaped nose, he's armed with an **icy stick**. You spin round to the south door but find that too blocked by a lumbering goblin guard.

"Kill them!" spits the wheezing goblin to his comrade.
Go to 182

37

"I'm betting this is no ordinary **chisel**," says Kyla, snatching it from your hand and starting work trying to release one of the **blue shields**. "I bet we'll soon be able to - *aha!*"

One of the **blue shields** breaks free from the plaque. However, the **chisel** snaps in two.

"Damn! Thought we'd be able to get them all off with this. Oh, well. Look what we *have* got!"

Choose whether you or **Kyla** *take the* **blue shield**. *Remember each of you can only carry no more than six items at once. Deduct the* **chisel** *from your items list.*

Maybe you'll find a way to get the other items later. Now, there is nothing left to examine in the gallery, so you turn toward the exits.

If you make your way toward the north door, go to 36
If you leave by the south door, go to 431

38

"Oh, I quite understand," dribbles a low shelf shaved head. "I was silly to ask."

"Did you say you're looking for Ember?" checks black beard.

Kyla tells him you are.

"K... k... keep n... north," advises a top shelf head with a stammer.

"Old Ember, eh?" reminisces one head with a monocle in one eye. "Hmm! Safe journey, friend!"

If you make your way toward the north door, go to 426
If you go back through the easy door, go to 237

39

Everything is pitch black. You ache all over. Did you hit the ground? You don't remember making impact. Did you knock yourself out? Did you survive the fall?

Unable to see, you realise you are now lying on cold, stone floor. There is no sound. You spread out your hands, fumbling blindly. You hear your own fingers move about you, like scurrying rats in the dark. Unable to find a wall or ledge to hold, you carefully rise to your feet. You feel dizzy. Woozy.

Then there is light. It beats from the centre of a giant three headed slug. It is moving towards you. The head closest to you bulges transparent with speckled blue liquid, bloated and stretched. The next resembles a blood blister about to burst, deep crimson, throbbing. Furthest from you is the smallest head, pulsing a deep, neon glow.

The three heads advance with giant, gnashing jaws.

Go to 458

40

Kyla attacks Headless Figure.

Headless Figure successfully defends himself with the **blue shield**.

Headless Figure is unaffected.

Headless Figure raises the **purple stick** and casts a **'DEEP BOLT'** spell on you.

Bang! A stunning hit.

You are bleeding.

Go to 453

41

The cabinet's made of very thick glass. Inside there's a **metal**

club, a **chisel**, a **bone** and **2 glittered pebbles**. There is no lid or visible way to open it up.

Kyla slams her fist down upon it but it does not break.

With no way of yet opening the glass cabinet, you cannot get to these items at the moment.

If you look at the plaque, go to 321
If you make your way to the north door, go to 10
If you leave by the south door, go to 431

42
If you examine the body of the goblin, go to 488
If you look in the larder door, go to 94
If you leave by the north door, go to 475
If you leave by the south door, go to 206

43
The **knitted puppet** chuckles.

"So you say, so you say. Can you see the colours of a goblin's scales? See what colour my skin is, eh? Tell me, what colour scales would we never see on a goblin?"

If you say black scales, go to 501
If you say brown scales, go to 428

44
"Hey, don't speak to us like-"

"It's all right, Kyla. Here's your **wooden bucket**."

For a moment there is silence. Then, a quiet 'pop', and the bubble has disappeared.

"What's going on?" Kyla looks up and down the field. "Did bubble die?"

"I'm in here, nincompoop!"

Inside the **wooden bucket**, a small puddle of water is now insulting you!

Kyla peers into the pail to address the burst bubble.

"Listen, you," she orders. "We've survived a fight with the

Queen elf, so we can survive a fight with a puddle, OK? Look, we're trying to find the wizard Ember. Can you help us?"

"Oh," the burst bubble continues in a quite different tone. "Any enemy of Lyric's is a friend of mine. OK, you want to find Ember? Be ready to fight. Really fight. You'll need weapons. I will go with you into battle. Hurry! Take me south in this **wooden bucket** to goat girl's shop. Now!"

If you decide to take burst bubble with you, make a note of the new item **wooden bucket**.

If you leave by the north portal, go to 135
If you leave by the east portal, go to 390
If you leave by the south portal, go to 123

45

Before stepping through the door, Kyla unrolls the **flying carpet**. It is just big enough for you both to stand upon. Gritting your teeth, you push through the pine door and into the portal.

True to the headless wizard's word, the **flying carpet** takes both your weight, and you sail steadily through the liozard's insides. Good job you had the **flying carpet** this time, as where there was a platform earlier is now a deep lake of stomach acid. The decapitated head of the half-digested goblin bobs up and down on its surface.

"Look, there's the other portal."

"That's lucky," Kyla replies. "The **flying carpet** is starting to lose height. Here we go!"

Together you pass safely though the portal and into the big steel corridor. The **flying carpet** makes a smooth landing and you dismount.

Its power now gone, you can either discard this item or keep it as a **thin carpet**. *If you want to keep the* **thin carpet** *note the change on your item list.*

The steel trunk still sits by the west wall. The barred

window is just beside it.

If you open the trunk, go to 50

If you look through the window, go to 19

If you leave by the north door, go to 193

If you leave by the east door, go to 450

If you leave by the portal in the south wall, go to 293

46

Kyla attacks White Bearded Man.

Kyla misses!

White Bearded Man is unaffected.

White Bearded Man attacks Kyla.

White Bearded Man misses!

Kyla is unaffected.

You attacks White Bearded Man.

Crack! A successful hit.

White Bearded Man collapses, exhausted.

White Bearded Man drops **lucky charm**.

If you want to keep it, note you have gained a **lucky charm**.

Go to 97

47

This shiny corridor is made entirely of steel. Thin electric lights line the ceiling. There are two solid metal doors in the north and east walls and a small, black portal in the south. There's a steel trunk and large barred window to the west.

If you open the trunk, go to 223

If you look through the window, go to 72

If you leave by the north door, go to 514

If you leave by the east door, go to 450

If you leave by the portal in the south wall, go to 208

48

You untie and read the **scroll tied with string**.

"I, the wizard Ember, have foreseen your plight, brave ones. Adrienne is alive! Keep heading north. Find an item with which to battle a spectral warrior. Beware of goblins! To aid your advance, I give you a single use of the '**DEEP MIRAGE**' spell. This unusual spell can be cast without a special wand. Use it to confuse the enemy. Stay strong against Lyric, comrades, for I will meet you soon... Ember."

Deduct **scroll tied with string** *from your items as you will not need it again. Note that you can now cast the* **DEEP MIRAGE** *spell one time only. Knowing this spell does not count towards your list of items. Once it's cast it can't be used again.*

With nothing else of interest here, you turn to the exits.

If you leave by the north door, go to 164

If you leave by the west door, go to 525

If you leave by the south door, through which you came, go to 190

49

You attack Hob Goblin.

You miss!

Hob Goblin is unaffected.

Hob Goblin raises the **purple stick** and casts a '**DEEP BOLT**' spell on Kyla.

Bang! A stunning hit.

Kyla collapses, exhausted.

You move next.

Go to 204

50

The trunk is empty.

If you look through the window, go to 19

If you leave by the north door, go to 193

If you leave by the east door, go to 450

If you leave by the portal in the south wall, go to 293

51

You invoke the spirit of Ember and slice at Lyric with **cobra sceptre!**

Smash! An outstanding hit.

Lyric is bleeding.

Lyric attacks you.

Bang! A stunning hit.

Cobra bracelet is caught by the **golden lance**. **Cobra bracelet** snaps in two.

You can no longer use **cobra bracelet** to travel through time.

You are bleeding.

If you have a gold ring, multiply the stars by the planets and go to that panel

If you do not have a gold ring, go to 465

52

Inside you discover an **icy stick**.

"Wow, what a weapon!" remarks Kyla. "If we run into Lyric again we'll need all we can to defend ourselves. This is some find!"

*If you decide to keep it, add the **icy stick** to your list of items. Note: You can use the **icy stick**. However, Kyla is too weak to use this*

item, as she is wounded from her earlier encounter with Lyric.
Go to 97

53

You return to the previously upside down room. It is still the right way up!
If you leave by the north door, go to 164
If you leave by the west door, go to 525
If you leave by the south door, go to 190

54

"Do you go down into the sewers?" you ask politely.

"Oh, yes, that's where you think I belong, the sewers," is the sorrowful response. "You'll be unhappy to hear that I don't. Dungeon level is as low as you go. Here is where I'm meant to say 'I'm going up', though the chance would be a fine thing." He pauses. "Because I'm so down."

"Yes, I got it," you reply.
If you ask elevator gargoyle to go up to the castle ground floor, go to 282
If you ask elevator gargoyle to go up to the tower, go to 347

55

Swift Elf raises the **purple stick** and casts a '**DEEP INFERNO**' spell on you, Sai, Kyla and Adrienne.

Smash! An outstanding hit.

Sai is bleeding.

Smash! An outstanding hit.

Kyla collapses, exhausted.

Smash! An outstanding hit.

Adrienne is bleeding.

Cobra shield flickers and the spirit of Ember wraps around your body!

You are unaffected.

If you want Sai to move next, go to 162
If you move next, go to 422

56

The white bearded man storms out of the gallery, leaving by the south exit.
If you look at the glass cabinet, go to 41
If you look at the plaque, go to 321
If you make your way to the north door, go to 10
If you leave by the south door, go to 431

57

Zuri attacks Rock Troll.

Bang! A stunning hit.

The **rock shield** cracks and snaps in two. Rock Troll can no longer use the **rock shield**.

Rock Troll is bleeding.

Rock Troll attacks Zuri.

Bang! A stunning hit.

The **rock shield** cracks and snaps in two. Zuri can no longer use the **rock shield**.

Zuri is bleeding.

You move next.
If you attack Rock Troll, go to 333
If you attack Cackling Goblin, go to 366

58

If you apply the green paste to her lips, go to 32
If you apply the purple paste to her lips, go to 461
If you change your mind and don't want to risk guessing, go to 97

59

Sai howls and lashes out with beak hands.

Handsome Elf successfully defends himself with the **golden**

shield.

Handsome Elf is unaffected.

Handsome Elf beats his chest and hollers for help.

Warty Goblin comes to his aid!

Warty Goblin attacks Sai.

Sai giggles and skips out of range.

Sai is unaffected.

You move next.

If you attack Handsome Elf, go to 375

If you attack Warty Goblin, go to 383

60

"I cannot fight alongside you, but I can equip you for the fight," she squeaks. "I still need more **glittered pebbles** so I can cast an important spell. If you have any, I'll gladly make an exchange!"

2 blue shields	1 glittered pebble
shiny whistle	1 glittered pebble
metal club	1 glittered pebble
purple glow	3 glittered pebbles
5 gold coins	3 glittered pebbles
scroll tied with string	7 glittered pebbles
cobra shield	10 glittered pebbles

If you choose to make any purchases note what they are and remember to deduct the appropriate number of **glittered pebbles**. *You may carry up to* **20 gold coins** *and, as they are so small, together they will count as only one item. Remember that Sai cannot carry or use items.*

"That's all I got," squeaks Fairy. "We're depending on you now. Don't let us down!"

Go to 518

61

You attack White Bearded Man.

You miss!

White Bearded Man is unaffected.

White Bearded Man attacks you.

White Bearded Man misses!

You are unaffected.

Kyla attacks White Bearded Man.

Crack! A successful hit.

White Bearded Man collapses, exhausted.

White Bearded Man drops **lucky charm**.

If you want to keep it, note you have gained a **lucky charm**.

Go to 97

62

On the table is a small, blood-stained note book. It is a goblin's diary. It reads: *'Morning, kill. Lunch, then kill. Brush teeth. Kill, then bed.'* There is nothing else of interest in this room.

If you leave by the north door, go to 99

If you leave by the west door, go to 390

If you leave by the south door, go to 475

63

"Ah... red lum!" sighs the sketched lips. "Yes, that salve mixed with the tertreiah leaves, that's how he did it. Ah, that feels good. Thank you so much."

"That's OK," says Kyla. "Do you think that red lum would do my injuries any good?"

"Yes, but I'm afraid there isn't enough left in the jar," admits the broken painted lady. "I don't have any more. Sorry. The wizard Ember would be able to heal you though. You should go find him."

"Thanks," you smile.

The painted mouth licks its newly restored lips.

"You've been much nicer to me than that mad old artist. You deserve these more than him." You hear a deep clicking sound from the glass cabinet. "Open the glass cabinet. Take what is inside. Then go find Ember. He will help you out."

If you look at the glass cabinet, go to 173
If you look at the plaque, go to 82
If you leave by the north door, go to 450
If you leave by the south door, go to 431

64

If you have a 'DEEP MIRAGE' spell and wish Kyla to cast it now, go to 21
Otherwise, go to 75

65

You follow Sai into a large, light hall, made from thin pieces of timber hammered together in long, vertical lines. A number of creatures are in this hall, mostly huddled around a long beechwood chest in the centre of the room. A tall, slender elf looks up from the crowd.

"Sai! Hey, everyone, it's Sai!"

"Hey, Sai!" roars a gnarled tree lady, and soon the whole group are chatting with your friend.

Two doors lead out this hall, one west and one south. An elevator gargoyle shaft is in the north wall.

If you speak to the tall elf, go to 288
If you speak to the walking tree lady, go to 271
If you speak to the stumpy female goblin, go to 481
If you speak to the skinny female goblin, go to 491
If you speak to Fairy, go to 228
If you speak to the female magitright, go to 238
If you speak to the goat boy, go to 479
If you step onto the elevator gargoyle, go to 291
If you make your way to the west door, go to 505
If you make your way to the south door, go to 298

66

"Oi, put me back, big hands. I'm not done!"

Startled, you drop the **knitted puppet** back in the pot. Though it seems to be speaking to you, it has no mouth that you can see, just two round button eyes.

"That's right, smelly, some of us have baths round here, right? Now bog off, I want to relax."

If you obey the knitted puppet's wishes, go to 167
If you pester it some more, go to 336

67

"Bah!" grumbles the **knitted puppet**. "Here's where your lucky streak ends, my colour blind nemesis! Tell me the colour of this purple sock?"

If you say purple, go to 415
If you say something else, go to 86

68

Thick walls of chunky gold brick surround you. The ceiling above is made of thousands of tiny, gold spikes. The floor is all black and white marble tiles, resembling a chess board. Next to a large, steel trunk stands a slender, good looking elf boy. Blue-skinned and dressed in tight, silver armour, he points a **purple stick** at you and lets out a long, reedy laugh.

"Is this it? The great Rebellion? Should our Queen fear a couple of puny halflings such as you? Pa! Tomorrow, my friends, I will be leading our troops into war, to take this whole land by force. You're either with us or against us. What's it to be, halflings? Ready to meet your doom?"

Go to 108

69

You attack Headless Figure.

Headless Figure successfully defends himself with the **blue shield**.

Headless Figure is unaffected.

Headless Figure raises the **purple stick** and casts a '**DEEP BOLT**' spell on you.

Bang! A stunning hit.

You are bleeding.

Go to 453

70

"Stomach acid!" Kyla realises with a sudden fear. "We're going to get burned alive!"

Getting down on your knees, you start to rub the **soap** into the monster's stomach. As you quicken your scrubs, it begins to wobble underneath you, then slowly begin to descend.

"It's working. It's going to chuck us up! Hold on!"

Ping! The stomach floor springs back and shoots you both upward and into the portal above.

*Take the **soap** off of your list of items, as it cannot be used again.*

Go to 497

71

"Reckon you're clever? Reckon again! In the chamber of flesh, what colour are the eyes?"

If you say green, go to 198

If you say blue go to 452

72

Behind the barred window sits a young goat girl.

"Hey there!" she greets. "If you have any **gold coins**, I'll gladly make an exchange!"

golden lance	**2 gold coins**
golden shield	**2 gold coins**

"I have a new weapon just come in. It's a beauty! Wanna see it? It'll cost you **10 gold coins**."

*You don't have enough **gold coins**. You can't buy anything yet!*

"Nice to do business with you," she smiles. "See you again."

If you have a wooden bucket and wish to use it, go to 304
If you look in the trunk, go to 223
If you leave by the north door, go to 514
If you leave by the east door, go to 450
If you leave by the portal in the south wall, go to 208

73

Inside the doorway of this hut sits a young elf man. His arm is wrapped in a bloody bandage.
If you have a gold ring, go to 292
If not, but you do have a silver ring, go to 266
If you have neither of these items, go to 259

74

"Rubbish!" **knitted puppet** sniffs. "You're full of it, aren't you? Disgusting."

"What is it about being colour blind that gets to you like this?" asks Kyla. "Do you wish your doll was a bit brighter coloured or something?"

"I am not a doll, I am a collectable! Look missy, you wanna find Ember, you're gonna have to fight your way to him. Your little run in with Lyric, that's only the start of it. Get yourself some weapons from my mate Fairy. I'll give you a little something you can use to strike a deal with her. Look in my hand. No, not my puppet hand, my real hand, idiot! Go up to the castle level and keep west. Go on, get out of it, before I change my mind!"

Thanking **knitted puppet,** you turn away from the cauldron and look toward to the north door.
Go to 199

75

Kyla attacks Itchy Goblin.
Kyla misses!
Itchy Goblin is unaffected.
Drooling Goblin attacks Kyla.

Crack! A successful hit.

Kyla collapses, exhausted.

Yawning Goblin rushes forward.

Yawning Goblin attacks you.

Crack! A successful hit.

The **blue shield** cracks and snaps in two. You can no longer use the **blue shield**.

Itchy Goblin rushes forward.

Itchy Goblin attacks you.

Crack! A successful hit.

You are bleeding.

Go to 181

76

Drooling Goblin attacks Yawning Goblin.

Crack! A successful hit.

Yawning Goblin collapses, exhausted.

Itchy Goblin attacks Drooling Goblin.

Itchy Goblin misses!

Drooling Goblin attacks Itchy Goblin.

Crack! A successful hit.

Itchy Goblin collapses, exhausted.

Go to 467

77

"Ugh! Get away from me. Disgusting. All your kind should be shot! Go on, get out of it. Now!"

Go to 42

78

Yawning Goblin rushes forward.

Yawning Goblin attacks you.

Crack! A successful hit.

The **blue shield** cracks and snaps in two. You can no longer use the **blue shield**.

Itchy Goblin rushes forward.

Itchy Goblin attacks you.

Crack! A successful hit.

You are bleeding.

Go to 181

79

If you apply the red paste to her lips, go to 195

If you apply the purple paste to her lips, go to 461

If you change your mind and don't want to risk guessing, go to 97

80

If you have a 'DEEP MIRAGE' spell and you wish to cast it now, go to 21

Otherwise, go to 115

81

You take over the jar and rub the paste upon the broken painted lady's lips.

"Wh- what?" A pink tongue darts from the drawing and licks a small bit of the mixture you're applying. "It... it burns! Ugh, no! That's not the right one! What have you done to me? Help!"

"What have you done?" snaps Kyla. "Look, she's in agony! Come on, we should go."

If you hurry out the north door, go to 450
If you escape through the south door, go to 431
If you try slapping one of the other pastes on the broken painted lady, go to 130

82

Attached to the plaque are two **golden lances,** lay one over the other forming a cross. Beneath them, two **blue shields** have been stuck, forming a sort of coat of arms. Both you and Kyla try to prize the weapons off the plaque, but they seem to be stuck not with glue but sorcery.

With no way of yet releasing them from the plaque, you cannot take any of these items at the moment.
If you look at the glass cabinet, go to 173
If you leave by the north door, go to 450
If you leave by the south door, go to 431

83

The body is covered in a thick layer of dust. Its skin is dark green. There is definitely no sign of life. Kyla opens the goblin's hand and finds inside a cloth pouch containing **5 glittered pebbles**.

The pouch can carry more **glittered pebbles** *should you find and want to keep them - this pouch can hold up to* **20 glittered pebbles** *and they will still count as only one item. If you decide you want to keep it, decide who will carry the pouch (remember you can only carry 6 items each).*
If you look in the larder door, go to 84
If you leave by the north door, go to 451
If you leave by the south door, go to 206

84

Inside are a great number of tins and bottles of powders and pastes, many with damp or peeling labels describing their contents in an unknown text. One box contains nothing but glass tubes full of green eyeballs. Another contains a rolled up piece of parchment, *'Recipe For Red Sock Casserole'*. A big cardboard carton contains a dozen jars of extra **salted spinach**.

If you want, you can take one jar or more of extra **salted spinach**. *However, remember you and Kyla can only carry a maximum of six items each. Each jar counts as one item. If you decide to take any* **salted spinach**, *note how many you take on your item lists.*

Nothing else inside worth investigating, you close the larder door.

If you leave by the north door, go to 451
If you leave by the south door, go to 206

85

The body is covered in a thick layer of dust. Its skin is dark green. There is definitely no sign of life. Kyla opens the goblin's hand and finds inside a cloth pouch containing **5 glittered pebbles**.

The pouch can carry more **glittered pebbles** *should you find and want to keep them. This pouch can hold up to* **20 glittered pebbles** *and they will still count as only one item. If you decide you want to keep it, decide who will carry the pouch (remember you can only carry 6 items each).*

If you leave by the north door, go to 451
If you leave by the south door, go to 206

86

"Meh! Whatever," **knitted puppet** sulks.

"Ha ha!" gloats Kyla. "We proved you wrong, didn't we? Admit it! I got to say though, your attitude towards colour blind people is weird. Where does that even come from?"

"Shut up! Shut up!" yells **knitted puppet**. "Look, you wanna find Ember, right? You'll need to go up to the castle level before you can go down to the sewer. Find an elevator gargoyle. He'll be a bit grumpy at first, but then they always are. Oh, and watch out for Dream Molluscs."

Thanking **knitted puppet,** you turn away from the cauldron and look toward to the north door.
Go to 199

87

You attack Hob Goblin.

Crack! A successful hit.

The **blue shield** cracks and snaps in two. Hob Goblin can no longer use the **blue shield**.

Hob Goblin is bleeding.

Hob Goblin raises the **purple stick** and casts a 'DEEP BOLT' spell on Kyla.

Bang! A stunning hit.

Kyla collapses, exhausted.

You move next.
If you use a metal club, go to 436
If you use an icy stick, go to 204

88

Attached to the plaque are two **golden lances**, lay one over the other forming a cross. Beneath them two **blue shields** have been stuck, forming a sort of coat of arms. Both you and Kyla try to prize the weapons off the plaque, but they seem to be stuck not with glue but sorcery.

With no way of yet releasing them from the plaque, you cannot take any of these items at the moment.
Go to 97

89

You brandish the **purple glow** and wrap Mollusc Head in a distorted aura.

Crack! A successful hit.

Mollusc Head moans.

Mollusc Head holds its breath and vibrates.

Furthest Mollusc Head bursts in a slimy shower!

You are coated in thick goo.

Mollusc Head roars and vomits projectile acid.

Smash! An outstanding hit.

The **purple glow** implodes in thick yellow gas. You can no longer use the **purple glow**.

You are bleeding.

You attack closest Mollusc Head, go to 14

90

"Kyla is dead, but I don't believe Adrienne is. We must find Ember."

"How am I meant to climb a ladder with these?" Sai holds up his arms. "Anyway, the Rebellion is stronger now than when Ember led us. Maybe I'm not sure now whether he is the answer to all this. As for Adrienne... you don't really think she's alive? She's gone. You will be too if you go back there."

If you start to climb down the ladder without Sai, go to 332

If you change your mind, go to 473

91

Attached to the plaque are two **golden lances,** lay one over the other forming a cross. Beneath them two **blue shields** have been stuck, forming a sort of coat of arms. Both you and Kyla try to prize the weapons off the plaque, but they seem to be stuck not with glue but sorcery.

With no way of yet releasing them from the plaque, you cannot take any of these items at the moment.

Go to 17

92

You successfully defend yourself with the **blue shield**.

You are unaffected.

If you want Kyla to move first, go to 140

If you want to move first, go to 229

93

"Damn colour blind freaks! Taking over our dungeon, thinking they're like us!" gags the **knitted puppet**. "They make me wanna wretch! So, you're asking for my help? Reckon you're not colour blind, do you? You sure look like a colour blinder to me. But if you're not, you won't mind proving it. You had a fight with Lyric? Tell me the colour of the Queen elf's armour. If you can see it, that is!"

If you say she wears golden armour, go to 43

If you say she wears silver armour, go to 196

If you don't want to play the knitted puppet's games, go to 77

94

Inside are a great number of tins and bottles of powders and pastes, many with damp or peeling labels describing their contents in an unknown text. One box contains nothing but glass tubes full of green eyeballs. Another contains a rolled up piece of parchment, *'Recipe For Fairy Wing Pie'*. A big cardboard carton contains a dozen jars of extra **salted spinach**.

If you want, you can take one jar or more of extra **salted spinach** *with you, however remember you and Kyla can only carry a maximum of six items each. Each jar counts as one item. If you decide to take any* **salted spinach***, note how many you take on your item lists.*

Nothing else inside worth investigating, you close the larder door.

Go to 42

95

If you bought the scroll tied with string, go to 48 if you want to untie it now

If you don't have or don't want to unwrap this item yet, go to 470

96

You attack Muttering Goblin.

Crack! A successful hit.

Muttering Goblin is bleeding.

Dribbling Goblin attacks Sai.

Sai giggles and skips out of range.

Sai is unaffected.

Sai moves next.

If you want Sai to attack Dribbling Goblin, go to 111

If you want Sai to attack Muttering Goblin, go to 250

97

If you look at the glass cabinet, go to 147

If you look at the plaque, go to 88

If you leave by the north door, go to 450

If you leave by the south door, through which you came, go to 431

98

"Stop!" cries the goat boy. "They're innocent. Take me instead."

"Oh, I will take you, Filth," sneers the Queen elf. "I will

take you all!"

Driving her **golden lance** at your head, it plunges straight through your right eye, which bursts like a split olive.

"I overestimated you," the Queen elf sighs, ripping her **golden lance** from your brain, then smashing it into your chest. "You're worth nothing to me."

She wrenches the **golden lance** out of your body, sending you flailing to the ground, gasping for breath and pawing at the gooey mess pulled from your eye socket down across your face. Pain quickly overwhelms you. You are vaguely aware of the heavy crunch of Kyla's and Adrienne's twisted bodies collapsing beside you as the Queen elf continues to wreak her devastation.

Go to 194

99

"Hey, we've come to an elevator room!" cheers Kyla.

Sure enough, a circular, orange brick shaft stands directly in front of you in the north wall. There are no other doors other than the one through which you just came. To your left is a padlocked cupboard. Beside it is a steel trunk. The entrance to the elevator is open but no elevator is inside.

"Hello?" you call up the shaft, but get no reply. You see no button or lever for the elevator.

If you look in the trunk, go to 103
If you leave by the south door, go to 209

100

"Goblins?" echoes a woman's voice about the gallery, and suddenly the whole room grows a little darker. "More of Lyric's cronies? Who do you think you are, breaking into my gallery? Fight!"

Go to 23

101

You attack Wheezing Goblin.

Crack! A successful hit.

Wheezing Goblin is bleeding.

Wheezing Goblin attacks you.

Wheezing Goblin misses!

You are unaffected.

Lumbering Goblin rushes forward.

Lumbering Goblin attacks Kyla.

Lumbering Goblin misses!

Kyla is unaffected.

Go to 100

102

Kyla raises the **purple stick** and casts a **'DEEP INFERNO'** spell on Clawed Dragon and Lyric.

The spell has no affect on Clawed Dragon.

Smash! An outstanding hit.

Lyric is bleeding.

Clawed Dragon spews a ball of fire at you.

You are engulfed in a blaze.

The **purple glow** implodes in thick yellow gas. You can no longer use the **purple glow**.

You are bleeding.

Lyric leaps down from Clawed Dragon's back.

Go to 159

103

There are two items in the trunk. One is a jar labelled **bottle of space**. An instruction beneath is advises to *'use liberally to de-animate the undead'*. The other item is a scroll. You unroll it and read: *'The Dream Mollusc cannot harm you when you are awake. Do not sleep! Stay awake tonight.'*

    If you decide to keep it, make a note of the **bottle of space**, *remembering that you and Kyla can carry a maximum of only six items each.*

Nothing else to see here, you leave by the door you came in by.

Go to 209

104

Sai howls and lashes out with beak hands.

Crack! A successful hit.

The **blue shield** cracks and snaps in two. Muttering Goblin can no longer use the **blue shield**.

Muttering Goblin is bleeding.

Muttering Goblin raises the **purple stick** and casts a '**DEEP HEAL**' spell on himself.

Muttering Goblin is fine.

You move next.

If you attack Dribbling Goblin, go to 440

If you attack Muttering Goblin, go to 96

105

For a long time, you do not move.

It's your fault. Kyla was hurt the moment she came to this hell-hole and how did you protect her?

It's Adrienne's fault. It was her obsession that first brought you here. How dare she let herself get captured by Lyric? Idiot!

No, it's Filth's fault. You wouldn't even be here if it wasn't for that stupid goat boy.

It's Lyric's fault. She commands the goblin hordes. Like the Hob goblin you have killed.

You have killed. That sentence repeats over and over inside your head. You have killed.

It is the dungeon's fault. This sick, soulless place turns everyone into monsters. Including you.

And Adrienne? Kyla is gone, but Adrienne still could be alive. Your stomach clenches when you imagine telling Adrienne that her lover is dead. You can't think like that. You are all alone now. You have to be strong. If Adrienne is still alive, you could be her only hope. You must pull yourself together. You have to find help. You have to find Ember.

Go to 261

106

Sai howls and lashes out with beak hands.

Bang! A stunning hit.

The **golden shield** is crushed to dust. Lyric can no longer use the **golden shield**.

Lyric is bleeding.

Go to 159

107

Inside are a great number of tins and bottles of powders and pastes, many with damp or peeling labels describing their contents in an unknown text. One box contains nothing but glass tubes full of green eyeballs. Another contains a rolled up piece of parchment, '*Recipe For Hob Goblin Head Roast With Parsnips And Peas*'. A big cardboard carton contains a dozen jars of extra **salted spinach**.

If you want you can take one jar or more of extra **salted spinach.** *However, remember you and Kyla can only carry six items each. Each jar counts as one item. If you decide to take* any **salted spinach***, note how many you take.*

Nothing else inside worth investigating, you close the larder door.

Go to 190

108

✎ **Fight!**

Handsome Elf   (Weapons: **purple stick / golden shield**)

Handsome Elf raises the **purple stick** and casts a '**DEEP INFERNO**' spell on you and Sai.

If you have a purple glow, go to 278

If you do not have a purple glow, but you have a blue shield, go to 395

If you have neither, go to 6

109

You attack Fire Troll.

Crack! A successful hit.

The **purple stick** cracks and snaps in two. Fire Troll can no longer use the **purple stick**.

Fire Troll collapses, exhausted.

Fire Troll drops **4 glittered pebbles**.

*You can hold up to **20 glittered pebbles** and together they will still count as only one item. If you want to keep them, note you have gained **4 glittered pebbles**.*

Rock Troll beats his chest and hollers for help.

Cackling Goblin comes to his aid!

Cackling Goblin attacks you.

Cackling Goblin misses!

You are unaffected.

Rock Troll attacks Zuri.

Zuri successfully defends himself with the **rock shield**.

Zuri is unaffected.

Zuri moves next.

If you want Zuri to attack Rock Troll, go to 57

If you want Zuri to attack Cackling Goblin, go to 361

110

You invoke the spirit of Ember and slice at Lyric with **cobra sceptre**!

Smash! An outstanding hit.

Lyric is bleeding.

Lyric attacks you.

Bang! A stunning hit.

Cobra bracelet is caught by the **golden lance**. **Cobra bracelet** snaps in two. You can no longer use **cobra bracelet** to travel through time.

You are bleeding.

If you have a gold ring, multiply the stars by the planets and go to that panel

If you do not have a gold ring, go to 391

111

Sai howls and lashes out with beak hands.

Crack! A successful hit.

Dribbling Goblin is bleeding.

Muttering Goblin raises the **purple stick** and casts a '**DEEP HEAL**' spell on Dribbling Goblin.

Dribbling Goblin is fine.

Go to 502

112

Kyla attacks Half-digested Goblin.

Crack! A successful hit.

Half-digested Goblin collapses, exhausted.

Half-digested Goblin drops **2 glittered pebbles**.

You can hold up to **20 glittered pebbles** *and together they will still count as only one item. If you want to keep them, note you have gained* **2 glittered pebbles**.

Go to 185

113

⚔ Fight!

Rock Troll   (Weapons: **rock club / rock shield**)
Fire Troll   (Weapons: **purple stick / rock shield**)
Zuri   (Weapons: **Roxcalibur / rock shield**)

Fire Troll raises the **purple stick** and casts a '**DEEP BOLT**' spell on you.
If you have a purple glow, go to 326
If not, go to 134

114
If you have cobra sceptre, go 447
If you do not have cobra sceptre, go to 377

115

You attack Drooling Goblin.
Drooling Goblin successfully defends himself with the **blue shield**.
Drooling Goblin is unaffected.
Drooling Goblin attacks you.
Drooling Goblin misses!
You are unaffected.
Go to 78

116
The inside is empty, except for a small Fairy. There are two exits, a south door and an east door.
    "Hey there!" she squeaks. "Do you have any **glittered pebbles**? I collect **glittered pebbles** to use for my spells. If you have any **glittered pebbles**, I'll gladly make an exchange!"

Jar of **salted spinach**	**1 glittered pebble**
tin box	**1 glittered pebble**
packet of **icing sugar**	**1 glittered pebble**
blue shield	**1 glittered pebble**
metal club	**3 glittered pebbles**
purple glow	**6 glittered pebbles**
1 gold coin	**8 glittered pebbles**
cobra shield	**15 glittered pebbles**

You can take as many items as you can carry (remember, you can carry up to six items and no more) as long as you have the right number of **glittered pebbles** *to make the exchange. If you can't afford an item, you can't have it! However, if you have enough* **glittered pebbles** *to buy more than one of any item, up to ten of each are available. If you choose to make any purchases, note what they are and remember to deduct the appropriate number of* **glittered pebbles***.*

"Nice to do business with you," squeaks Fairy. "See you again!"

Go to 246

117

Kyla attacks Sketched Lips.

Crack! A successful hit.

Sketched Lips are bleeding.

Sketched Lips shriek with rage and cast a **'DEEP BOLT'** spell on you.

Bang! A stunning hit.

You collapse, exhausted

Go to 34

118

You attack Muttering Goblin.

Crack! A successful hit.

The **blue shield** cracks and snaps in two. Muttering Goblin can no longer use the **blue shield**.

Muttering Goblin is bleeding.
Dribbling Goblin attacks Sai.
Sai giggles and skips out of range.
Sai is unaffected.
Sai moves next.
If you want Sai to attack Dribbling Goblin, go to 111
If you want Sai to attack Muttering Goblin, go to 250

119

⚔ Fight!

White Bearded Man   (Weapons: **icy stick**)

If you want Kyla to move first, go to 46
If you want to move first, go to 61

120

As you are leaving Zuri's home you notice something shining in the grass. You stoop down to see a small **silver whistle**, half buried in the dirt. You pick it up, dust the earth from it, and blow. There is no sound. It does not seem to work.

*If you feel this item is worth keeping you can add a **silver** **whistle** to your list of items (remember you can only carry a maximum of six at once).*
If you look about the west-most hut, go to 463
If you look about the north-most hut, go to 116

121

Your attempt at an impossible choice makes you realise how similar to a dream your experiences are becoming. A dream. Colours around you swirl and merge and what feels like a heavy blanket presses against your body. Are you standing or lying down? You no longer know which way is up. You try to speak but your voice comes out in slow motion, unintelligibly slurred. You can't move your arms or legs. You are in a dream from which you can't awake.

A reedy voice rasps in your ear, "Liars and cheats get nowhere in these dark lands..."

Go to 194

122

You attack Armoured Skeletal Knight.

You miss!

Armoured Skeletal Knight is unaffected.

Go to 235

123

You are back in the big steel corridor.

If you look in the trunk, go to 486

If you look through the window, go to 487

If you leave by the north door, go to 137

If you leave by the east door, go to 450

If you leave by the portal in the south wall, go to 208

124

If you want Adrienne to attack Swift Elf, go to 364

If you want Adrienne to heal herself, go to 149

If you want Adrienne to heal Sai, go to 445

If you want Adrienne to heal Kyla, go to 274

If you want Adrienne to heal you, go to 175

125

You invoke the spirit of Ember and slice at Lyric with **cobra sceptre**!

Silence.

Then Lyric emits a piercing scream and dazzling light fills the room.

Lyric collapses, exhausted.

Go to 354

126

Clawed Dragon swoops!

Clawed Dragon spews a ball of fire at you.

Cobra shield flickers and the spirit of Ember wraps around your body!

You are unaffected.

Clawed Dragon soars up and out of range.

If you want Sai to move first, go to 192

If you want Kyla to move first, go to 233

If you move first, go to 322

127

To your surprise, instead of seeing a stew or broth brewing away inside the cauldron, it is a load of clothes that are being boiled! Interestingly, all the items in here are a dark, crimson red. There are no clothes of any other colour inside. However, amongst the vests, shorts and socks, a black **knitted puppet** is floating on the surface. Also in the cauldron is a long, metal ladle.

If you use the ladle to spoon out an item of clothing, go to 144

If you use the ladle to spoon out the knitted puppet, go to 66

If you turn your attention back to the rest of the room, go to 167

128

You invoke the spirit of Ember and slice at Massive Elf with **cobra sceptre**!

Massive Elf successfully defends himself with the **golden shield**.

Massive Elf is unaffected.

Go to 362

129

Behind the barred window sits a young goat girl.

"Hey there!" she greets. "If you have any **gold coins**, I'll gladly make an exchange!"

metal club	1 gold coin
golden lance	9 gold coins
golden shield	9 gold coins

You don't have any **gold coins***. You can't buy anything yet!*

"Nice to do business with you," she smiles. "See you again."

If you look in the trunk, go to 136

If you leave by the north door, go to 193

If you leave by the east door, go to 450

If you leave by the portal in the south wall, go to 179

130

If you apply the red paste to her lips, go to 461

If you apply the green paste to her lips, go to 32

If you change your mind and don't want to risk guessing, go to 97

131

You attack Sketched Lips.

Crack! A successful hit.

Sketched Lips are bleeding.

Sketched Lips shriek with rage and cast a **'DEEP BOLT'** spell on you.

Bang! A stunning hit.

You collapse, exhausted

Go to 34

132

⚔ Fight!

Rabid Goblin   (Weapons: **icy stick / blue shield**)

Rabid Goblin attacks you.

You are bathed in foggy light from the **purple glow**.

You are unaffected.

If you want Kyla to cast a spell, go to 327

If you want to attack, go to 318

133

If you want Sai to attack Massive Elf, go to 202
If you want Sai to attack Duke Elf, go to 412

134

Bang! A stunning hit!

You collapse, exhausted.

Go to 370

135

This portal is locked and you can't go through it yet.

Go to 137

136

The trunk has no items inside. However, a tiny Fairy, no bigger than your fingernail, flits out!

"Hey there!" squeaks Fairy. "Do you have any **glittered pebbles**? I collect **glittered pebbles** to use for my spells. If you have any **glittered pebbles**, I'll gladly make an exchange!"

Jar of **salted spinach**	1 glittered pebble
bottle of space	1 glittered pebble
blue shield	1 glittered pebble
lucky charm	2 glittered pebbles
metal club	5 glittered pebbles
purple glow	9 glittered pebbles

You can take as many items as you can carry (remember, each person can carry up to six items and no more) as long as you have the right number of **glittered pebbles** *to make the exchange. If you can't afford an item, you can't have it! However, if you have enough* **glittered pebbles** *to buy more than one of any item, up to ten of each are available. If you choose to make any purchases note what they are and remember to deduct the appropriate number of* **glittered pebbles**. *Note: You can use the* **metal club**, *however Kyla is too weak to carry this item yet, as she is still wounded from her earlier encounter with*

Lyric. Any of the other items can be carried by either of you.

"Nice to do business with you," squeaks Fairy. "See you again!" With that, she flits away.

If you look through the window, go to 129
If you leave by the north door, go to 193
If you leave by the east door, go to 450
If you leave by the portal in the south wall, go to 179

137

You are in the hologram garden with its three exit portals.
If you leave by the north portal, go to 135
If you leave by the east portal, go to 390
If you leave by the south portal, go to 47

138

You step outside into a huge grassy field, spreading out in each direction as far as the eye can see. Standing unsupported a little to your left is a rectangular dark portal. A third stands directly opposite.

"The hologram garden," nods Kyla, pushing her hand against what should be thin air. "Projected on invisible walls. Lyric is one strong witch. Even with **cobra sceptre**, can we really beat her?"

"Kyla, look behind you!"

From the same portal you entered by, a rabid goblin has emerged, fangs bared!

Go to 132

139

Kyla raises the **purple stick** and casts a **'DEEP INFERNO'** spell on Swift Elf, Clawed Dragon and Lyric.

Smash! An outstanding hit.

The **golden shield** is crushed to dust. Duke Elf can no longer use the **golden shield**.

Swift Elf is bleeding.

Clawed Dragon is out of range.

Clawed Dragon is unaffected.

Lyric is out of range.

Lyric is unaffected.

Go to 394

140

Kyla attacks Hob Goblin.

Hob Goblin successfully defends himself with the **blue shield**.

Hob Goblin is unaffected.

Hob Goblin raises the **purple stick** and casts a **'DEEP BOLT'** spell on Kyla.

Bang! A stunning hit.

Kyla collapses, exhausted.

You move next.

Go to 524

141

"Who's there?" you call out into the vast gallery, your words echoing round its towering walls.

"Who do you think?" the voice answers. "His 'broken painted lady'. I'm supposed to look like that murderous Lyric, how depressing is that? Fortunately for me I don't look like... well, let's be honest, I don't look like very much at all, do I?"

Finally you spot, high up on the south wall, a painting of a large green eye, occasionally blinking, looking down at you and Kyla. The second eye is in a separate frame, lower, to your right. Just above the cabinet, a pair of crudely drawn bright red lips are where the voice is coming from.

"You're alive?" gasps Kyla. "That's amazing!"

"More alive than you look," observes the broken painted lady, referring to Kyla's heavy wounds. "Did I hear you say Lyric did that? You were lucky to escape. Hmm. You seem to be listening to me more than that old fool who painted me ever does. Would you please do me a favour?"

If you say you will, go to 28

If you explain that you can't as you have to find Adrienne, go to 405

142

Duke Elf attacks you.

Crack! A successful hit.

You collapse, exhausted.

Go to 432

143

Crack! A successful hit.

You are bleeding.

Kyla attacks Brigadier Elf.

Kyla misses!

Brigadier Elf is unaffected.

Brigadier Elf attacks you.

Crack! A successful hit.

You collapse, exhausted.

Go to 448

144

You pull out a **wet sock**.

If you want to keep the **wet sock**, *add it to your list of items. Remember, Kyla and you can only carry up to six items each.*
Go to 167

145

You invoke the spirit of Ember and slice Massive Elf in half with **cobra sceptre**!

Massive Elf collapses, exhausted.

Massive Elf drops **6 glittered pebbles**.

If you want to keep them, note you have gained **6 glittered pebbles**.
Go to 16

146

Kyla raises the **purple stick** and casts a 'DEEP BOLT' spell on Fat Elf.

Fat Elf is bathed in foggy light from the **purple glow**.

Fat Elf is unaffected.

Whispering Elf reappears.

Whispering Elf beats her chest and hollers for help.

Cloaked Elf comes to her aid!

Cloaked Elf attacks you.

Bang! A stunning hit.

The **purple glow** implodes in thick yellow gas. You can no longer use the **purple glow**.

You are bleeding.
Go to 280

147

The cabinet's made of very thick glass. Inside there's a **metal club**, a **chisel**, a **bone** and **2 glittered pebbles**. There is no lid or visible way to open it up. Kyla slams her fist down upon it but it does not break.

With no way of yet opening the glass cabinet, you cannot get these items at the moment.
Go to 97

148

You invoke the spirit of Ember and slice at Lyric with **cobra sceptre**!

Silence.

Then Lyric emits a piercing scream and dazzling light fills the room.

Lyric collapses, exhausted.

Go to 224

149

Adrienne knows that she doesn't need healing yet. Choose someone else instead.

If you want Adrienne to heal Sai, go to 445

If you want Adrienne to heal Kyla, go to 274

If you want Adrienne to heal you, go to 175

If you want Adrienne to attack Swift Elf, go to 364

Or, if you want Sai to move next, go to 188

If you want Kyla to move next, go to 139

If you move next, go to 211

150

You are in a gallery. Light shines down through a giant stained glass window of the Queen elf high in the north wall. The rest of the room is filled floor to ceiling with golden framed paintings. Beside the dark oak door in the north wall is a glass cabinet.

If you look at the glass cabinet, go to 205

If you leave by the north door, go to 450

If you leave by the south door, go to 431

151

The cabinet's made of very thick glass. Inside there's a **metal club**, a **chisel**, a **bone** and **2 glittered pebbles**. There is no lid or visible way to open it up. Kyla slams her fist down upon it but it does not break.

With no way of yet opening the glass cabinet, you cannot get to these items at the moment.

Go to 17

152

You attack Dribbling Goblin.
You miss!
Dribbling Goblin is unaffected.
Dribbling Goblin attacks you.
Dribbling Goblin misses!
You are unaffected.
Sai howls and lashes out with beak hands.
Bang! A stunning hit.
Dribbling Goblin collapses, exhausted.
Dribbling Goblin drops **3 glittered pebbles**.
You can hold up to **20 glittered pebbles** *and together they will still count as only one item. If you want to keep them, note you have gained* **3 glittered pebbles**.

Go to 294

153

You invoke the spirit of Ember and slice at Duke Elf with **cobra sceptre**!
Duke Elf successfully defends himself with the **golden shield**.
Duke Elf is unaffected.

If you want Sai to move next, go to 192
If you want Kyla to move next, go to 521

154

⚔ Fight!

Armoured Skeletal Knight   (Weapons: **metal club / blue shield**)

Armoured Skeletal Knight attacks Sai.
Sai giggles and skips out of range.

Sai is unaffected.

If you want Sai to move first, go to 262

If you want to move first:

If you have a bottle of space and want to use it, go to 272

If you have a bottle of oil and want to use it, go to 121

If you have a bone and want to use it, go to 260

Otherwise, go to 122

155

Crack! A successful hit.

The **blue shield** cracks and snaps in two. You can no longer use the **blue shield**.

You are bleeding.

Kyla attacks Brigadier Elf.

Kyla misses!

Brigadier Elf is unaffected.

Brigadier Elf attacks you.

Crack! A successful hit.

You collapses, exhausted.

Go to 448

156

Smash! An outstanding hit.

Sai is bleeding.

Smash! An outstanding hit.

Kyla is bleeding.

Smash! An outstanding hit.

The **purple glow** implodes in thick yellow gas. You can no longer use the **purple glow**.

You are bleeding.

Go to 142

157

A deep, mechanical rumbling can be heard. Then, all about you, the room begins to quake. Kyla clings to your arm, although the platform on which your standing seems to be remaining stable.

With a long, groaning creak, the entire room begins to move! The ledge you're stood on appears to be the axis as the space starts to rotate! Slowly the whole place turns, until the roof becomes the wall, the wall becomes the floor, until finally everything is the right way up.

You are staring at Kyla in disbelief when a slight burst of light grabs your attention. A tiny Fairy, no bigger than your fingernail, has appeared at your side!

"Hey there!" squeaks Fairy. "Do you have any **glittered pebbles**? I collect **glittered pebbles** to use for my spells. If you have any **glittered pebbles**, I'll gladly make an exchange!"

scroll tied with string	**1 glittered pebble**
dry sock	**1 glittered pebble**
blue shield	**1 glittered pebble**
icy stick	**1 glittered pebble**
knitted puppet	**2 glittered pebbles**
metal club	**5 glittered pebbles**
purple glow	**8 glittered pebbles**

You can take as many items as you can carry (remember, each person can carry up to six items and no more) as long as you have the right number of **glittered pebbles** *to make the exchange. If you can't afford an item, you can't have it! However, if you have enough* **glittered pebbles** *to buy more than one of any item, up to ten of each are available. If you choose to make any purchases note what they are and remember to deduct the appropriate number of* **glittered pebbles**. *Note: You can use the* **icy stick** *or* **metal club** *as a weapon. However, Kyla is too weak to carry either of these items yet, as she is still wounded from her earlier encounter with Lyric. Any of the other items can be carried by either of you.*

"Nice to do business with you," squeaks Fairy. "See you again!" With that, she flits away.

Go to 95

158

Swift Elf raises the **purple stick** and casts a '**DEEP INFERNO**' spell on you, Sai, Kyla and Adrienne.

Smash! An outstanding hit.

Sai collapses, exhausted.

Smash! An outstanding hit.

Kyla is bleeding.

Smash! An outstanding hit.

Adrienne is bleeding.

Cobra shield flickers and the spirit of Ember wraps around your body!

You are unaffected.

If you want Kyla to move next, go to 176

If you move next, go to 388

159

Lyric attacks you.

Bang! A stunning hit.

The **purple glow** implodes in thick yellow gas. You can no longer use the **purple glow**.

You collapse, exhausted.

Go to 432

160

"Z... Zuri!" You are hardly able to speak. Sai told you he had died with the Rebellion.

"Freja saw to his wounds before she passed away," explains a tiny voice. Fairy flits into the tower.

Zuri says nothing. He stands over Lyric's fallen body, his eyes fixed upon your face.

"The Queen elf is dead. Yay!" squeals Fairy. "You really did it. Ember was right to trust you."

"But at what a cost..." you sigh. "So much death... I will never... ...."

"I think I have enough **glittered pebbles** now," interrupts Fairy, laying her **glittered pebbles** out in a large circle about Lyric's abuse suite. "Freja was teaching me how to heal. I'm too late for her, or the Rebellion, but with the magic of **glittered pebbles** combined in her teachings, I should be able to cast a '**DEEP HEAL**' so deep it can even cure recently deceased. Please, stand in this circle for me."

Go to 248

161

Adrienne raises the **purple stick** and casts a '**DEEP HEAL**' spell on Kyla.

Kyla is fine.

Go to 316

162

Sai howls and lashes out with beak hands.

Swift Elf successfully defends herself with the **golden shield**.

Swift Elf is unaffected.

Go to 234

163

Sai howls and lashes out with beak hands.

Crack! A successful hit.

The **golden shield** is crushed to dust. Duke Elf can no longer use the **golden shield**.

Duke Elf is bleeding.

Go to 362

164

You have discovered the sleeping quarters to a mob of goblins! One is sat at a small table, sharpening an **icy stick**. Another two leap out of wooden bunk beds upon seeing you. There are three exits from this room, but you are not able to escape through any of them until these servants of Lyric have been dealt with.

"Wanna join our slumber party?" slobbers the tallest and fattest of the three. "Say good night!"

Go to 471

165

You attack Bubble.

Pop! A successful hit.

Bubble bursts, exhausted.

Bubble drops **2 glittered pebbles**.

You can hold up to **20 glittered pebbles** *and together they will still count as only one item. If you want to keep them, note you have gained* **2 glittered pebbles**.

Go to 137

166

Swift Elf raises the **purple stick** and casts a **'DEEP INFERNO'** spell on you, Sai, Kyla and Adrienne.

Smash! An outstanding hit.

Sai collapses, exhausted.

Smash! An outstanding hit.

Kyla collapses, exhausted.

Smash! An outstanding hit.

Adrienne is bleeding.

Smash! An outstanding hit.

Cobra shield implodes in thick yellow gas. You can no longer use **cobra shield**.

You are bleeding.

Clawed Dragon swoops!

Lyric leaps down from Clawed Dragon's back.

Go to 159

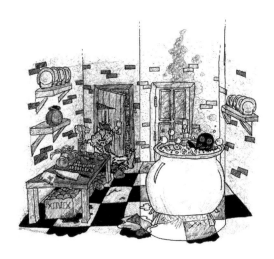

167

If you call out to see who spoke, go to 236
If you examine the body of the goblin, go to 478
If you look in the cauldron, go to 127
If you look in the larder door, go to 305
If you leave by the north door, go to 475
If you leave by the south door, go to 206

168

You brandish the **purple glow** and wrap Mollusc Head in a distorted aura.

Crack! A successful hit.

Mollusc Head moans.

Mollusc Head holds its breath and vibrates.

Closest Mollusc Head bursts in a slimy shower!

You are coated in thick goo.

With a slurping groan, the remaining heads swap places.

Mollusc Head growls and bubbles slime.

Mollusc Head inhales.

Mollusc Head growls and bubbles slime.

Mollusc Head inhales.

If you attack the closest Mollusc Head, go to 351
If you attack the furthest Mollusc Head, go to 516

169

Days go by. People hear of Lyric's death. At first, few grieve her passing, as so few outside the castle were aware of the full evil of her intent. However, when Fairy is chosen as successor, she chooses not to rule as Queen but as Dragon Claw Keep Protector. The monarchy's gold is redistributed amongst the people. Fairy elects Sai as Captain of the Guard and together they're hailed as heroes of a bright, new age. Fairy creates a wide ring of **glittered pebbles** around Dragon Claw Keep and casts a strong shielding spell to keep evil far away from this now blessed place.

You and Adrienne take work in the village farm, tending to crops and saving money to travel. Adrienne speaks little now and you work without word for most of the day. Your plan is to search the land for other mages, seek out one who has the power to reopen a portal and at last send you home.

You have become friendly with a young elf of the village by the name of Zuri. He was once part of the rebellion. Sai had thought him dead but Freja had managed to revive him before her own passing. Adrienne watches coldly as the two of you chat together across the corn field.

Nothing in your future seems certain anymore. You don't know if you'll ever see your old home, family or any of your friends again. But you live in hope that you will one day find a way back home.

170

Sai howls and lashes out with beak hands.
Sai misses!
Clawed Dragon is unaffected.
Go to 523

171

The man has not noticed you yet. Perhaps not surprising as he has no head!

If you want to attack the headless figure before he can attack you, go to 411

If you try speaking to him, go to 319

172

You lie beside Zuri, warm in his embrace. The bed covers are kicked onto the floor. You press your lips against his chest and close your eyes.

There has been no Queen since Lyric's death. Fairy has taken the role of Dragon Claw Keep Protector with Sai as Captain of the Guard. All the Queen elf's riches have been returned to the people, and a glorious new age of prosperity and happiness has spread throughout the land. You and Zuri have been working together on the farm. A year of growing and harvesting crops has gone by, and you are still as much in love as the day you first met. You think of Kyla and Adrienne often, wonder how they are doing, hope that they are well and happy.

Someone is shouting outside. Zuri rises, pulls on a shirt, and you too, quickly get dressed. Joining the elf outside you see Sai and Fairy, hurrying through the village, causing a great commotion.

"There they are, Sai!" calls Fairy. "Oh, listen - you won't believe it is true!"

"We have made a great discovery in the lower dungeons of Dragon Claw Keep," Sai reports. "Something truly remarkable."

"Go on," Zuri urges.

"Dragon eggs!" Fairy giggles. "Giant dragon eggs! And we thought Lyric had murdered all the dragons of the Keep. These eggs have been buried for years, but Sai thinks he knows how to hatch them. Imagine! Dragons at the Keep once more!"

"Dragons?" You wrap your arm around Zuri's waist. "Is that

safe?"

But Sai and Fairy are too excited to listen as they hurry off together to further spread the news. Zuri leads you back into your hut and together you start to make breakfast.

"Dragons, eh?" sighs Zuri. "I never thought a day like this would come in my lifetime."

Smiling, you place your hands on Zuri's shoulders and rest your head against his back. "You miss the adventure, don't you? There's a part of you aching to race into battle again."

Zuri chuckles. "You know me so well. I do sometimes miss the excitement."

Reaching into a trunk, you pull out **Roxcalibur** and hand Zuri his trusty blade. "There's nothing stopping us, you know. We could go travelling. There's always a land in need of heroes."

Zuri takes **Roxcalibur** from you and holds his sword up into the light. He looks deep in thought for a moment, then turns back to face you. You both smile. In this life, monsters and magic are always just around the next corner!

173

The cabinet's glass lifts off with ease. Inside there's a **metal club**, a **chisel**, a **bone** and **2 glittered pebbles**.

You can take as many items as you can carry, but remember, each person can carry up to six items and no more. However, you can carry up to **20 glittered pebbles** *(should you want to keep them) and, as they are so small, together they will still only count as one item. Note: You can use the* **metal club**, *but Kyla is too weak to carry this item yet, as she is still wounded from her earlier encounter with Lyric. Any of the other items can be carried by either of you.*

If you look at the plaque, go to 35
If you leave by the north door, go to 450
If you leave by the south door, go to 431

174

You attack Queen Elf.

Queen Elf successfully defends herself with the **golden shield**.

Queen Elf is unaffected.

Queen Elf attacks you.

Crack! A successful hit.

You are bleeding.

Go to 98

175

Adrienne raises the **purple stick** and casts a **'DEEP HEAL'** spell on you.

You are fine.

Go to 394

176

Kyla raises the **purple stick** and casts a **'DEEP INFERNO'** spell on Swift Elf, Clawed Dragon and Lyric.

Smash! An outstanding hit.

The **golden shield** is crushed to dust. Swift Elf can no longer use the **golden shield**.

Swift Elf collapses, exhausted.

Swift Elf drops **6 glittered pebbles**.

If you want to keep them, note you have gained **6 glittered pebbles**.

Clawed Dragon is out of range.

Clawed Dragon is unaffected.

Lyric is out of range.

Lyric is unaffected.

Clawed Dragon beats its chest and hollers for help.

Brute Elf comes to its aid!

Brute Elf attacks you.

Bang! A stunning hit.

Cobra shield implodes in thick yellow gas. You can no longer use **cobra shield**.

You are bleeding.
You invoke the spirit of Ember and slice Brute Elf in half with **cobra sceptre**!
Brute Elf collapses, exhausted.
Brute Elf drops **6 glittered pebbles**.
If you want to keep them, note you have gained **6 glittered pebbles**.
If you want Kyla to move next, go to 279
If you want Adrienne to move next, go to 197
If you move next, go to 256

177

You walk through the village graveyard. The sun's beginning to set and an evening chill pricks the air. A short, winding path leads between a small number of tombstones up to another entrance back into the castle. The gateway in is a large arch with a raised portcullis above it. You continue toward the castle, but Sai does not follow. Turning your head to see what is holding him up, you're amazed to see a large bony hand burst from the ground gripping his ankle! The ground around Sai now begins to split and quake as a giant skeletal warrior emerges from the earth beneath.

"I should have known, a spectral guardian!" Sai shakes his ankle free as the undead Goliath looms over you. "Brace yourself for attack!"
Go to 154

178

You brandish the **purple glow** and wrap Mollusc Head in a distorted aura.
Crack! A successful hit.
Mollusc Head moans.
Mollusc Head holds its breath and vibrates.
Closest Mollusc Head bursts in a slimy shower!
You are coated in thick goo.
With a slurping groan, the remaining heads swap places.

Mollusc Head growls and bubbles slime.
Mollusc Head inhales.
Mollusc Head growls and bubbles slime.
Mollusc Head inhales.
If you attack the closest Mollusc Head, go to 443
If you attack the furthest Mollusc Head, go to 516

179

Splat! You dive through the portal, back into the monster's gut. This time, however, you are not alone.

"Kyla, look out!"

From a deep pool of gunge to your left rises a zombie like creature, its skin acid scarred, its lipless mouth gibbering. The half-digested goblin groans, stumbles towards you, ready to attack!
Go to 180

180

✐ Fight!

Half-digested Goblin   (Weapons: **icy stick**)

Half-digested Goblin attacks you.
Half-digested Goblin misses!
You are unaffected.
If you have any new weapons / shields you may equip them here.
If you want Kyla to move first, go to 112
If you want to move first, go to 22

181

You're overpowered. The goblin's foam covered teeth are gnashing inches from your throat. The swampy stench on its breath makes you wretch. All items dropped, you now have both hands on its neck, trying to keep its jagged fangs away, but with its full body weight crushing down, you know your arms are about to give way any moment.

You shut your eyes. You scream.

Go to 194

182

✒ **Fight!**

Wheezing Goblin   (Weapons: **icy stick / blue shield**)

Lumbering Goblin   (Weapons: **icy stick / blue shield**)

Wheezing Goblin attacks you.

Wheezing Goblin misses!

You are unaffected.

If you have any new weapons / shields you may equip them here.

Lumbering Goblin is out of range.

If you want Kyla to move first, go to 27

If you want to move first, go to 101

183

Sai howls and lashes out with beak hands.

Sai misses!

Clawed Dragon is unaffected.

Clawed Dragon spews a ball of fire at you.

You are engulfed in a blaze.

The **purple glow** implodes in thick yellow gas. You can no longer use the **purple glow**.

You are bleeding.

Lyric leaps down from Clawed Dragon's back.

Go to 159

184

The headless wizard's body turns as you and Kyla fall through the door and collapse onto the floor of his marble walled home. The cabinets of heads *tut* and whisper their disapproval. The headless

wizard's body stands, walks over to you and helps you back up.
If you have something you would like to offer the wizard, go to 466
If you want to attack the wizard, go to 411
If neither of the above apply, go to 455

185
Your foe slumps back, already beaten before the battle began. Any weapons or shields you had prior to the encounter are still intact. However, the force of the combat has twisted the beast's innards back into contraction. Once again you are being spat out!
Go to 184

186
"Wake up! Hey, you've got to wake up!"

Someone is shaking you. Where are you? Did you fall asleep? You had a dream about... Ember! You bolt upright. Kyla is sat beside you. She looks different. Older. Confident. Her pink T-shirt gone, she now wears a starry purple gown. Your clothes have also changed. You are dressed in strong, purple metal armour. It is really uncomfortable! You rub your aching eyes and slowly stand.

"There are more gifts from Ember in these trunks," Kyla enthuses. "Come on, we've got to go!"

Back in the dungeon, you are beside the hole down to the sewers. The ladder is gone. The cage that barred entry to the steel trunks has also disappeared. Kyla is bursting with excitement. You had barely got used to her death and so suddenly she is back, more energetic than ever.

"We can't hang about, we've got to find **cobra sceptre** before the elite guard!"

Kyla will now fight at your side!
If you open the first steel trunk, go to 372
If you open the second steel trunk, go to 368

187

Sai howls and lashes out with beak hands.

Crack! A successful hit.

The **golden shield** is crushed to dust. Lyric can no longer use the **golden shield**.

Lyric is bleeding.

Go to 496

188

Sai howls and lashes out with beak hands.

Swift Elf successfully defends herself with the **golden shield**.

Swift Elf is unaffected.

Go to 394

189

You take over the jar and rub the paste upon the broken painted lady's lips.

"Wh- what?" A pink tongue darts from the drawing and licks a small bit of the mixture you're applying. "It... it burns! Ugh, no! That's not the right one! What have you done to me? Help!"

"What have you done?" snaps Kyla. "Look, she's in agony! Come on, we should go."

If you hurry out the north door, go to 450
If you escape through the south door, go to 431
If you try slapping one of the other pastes on the broken painted lady, go to 79

190
You are in a bright but cluttered kitchen. On your left is series of tables, upon which are a variety of quite fresh looking vegetables and several sharp looking knives. To your right is a large bubbling cauldron. Above the cauldron, a long upward tunnel leads through the ceiling and day light pours through. There are cupboards and shelves on every wall.
If you look in the cauldron, go to 435
If you look in the larder door, go to 107
If you leave by the north door, go to 475
If you leave by the south door, go to 206

191
Adrienne attacks Queen Elf.
Queen Elf successfully defends herself with the **golden shield**.
Queen Elf is unaffected.
Queen Elf attacks Adrienne.
Crack! A successful hit.
Adrienne is bleeding.
Go to 438

192
If you want Sai to attack Duke Elf, go to 163
If you want Sai to attack Mysterious Elf, go to 241

193
You step out from a dark portal into a huge grassy field, spreading out in each direction as far as the eye can see. Blue, cloudless skies are overhead, the sun shining peacefully. A

wooden bucket lies at your feet. Standing unsupported by any wall a little to your right is another rectangular portal. A third stands directly opposite. You see the meadow continue either side of each portal, as if all three empty door frames have been placed in this countryside, their insides just coloured black, though by now you know a deeper magic will be at play.

"It's not real," exclaims Kyla, pushing her hand against what should be thin air. "This is an invisible wall. I think we're just in a normal room, the grass and skies are some sort of hologram."

"Kyla, look behind you!"

A giant bubble, about twice as tall as you are, is floating towards her. It is transparent, like its made from washing up liquid, but from somewhere deep within a low growl, more similar to the sound a wolf might make, can be heard.

Kyla backs away until she's pressed against the holographic wall.

If you try to attack the bubble, go to 290

If you try to communicate with it, go to 11

If you dive back through the portal from which you came, go to 47

194

A million dreams away, some childhood toys lie piled up in a flat which will, in a week or so's time, be found empty by its landlord. A mobile phone, sat next to three cold mugs of tea, has dozens of missed calls and texts.

"Adrienne? Where are you?"

Amongst the clutter of papers, dolls and damp clothes is a table, where a circle of candles have now burned out.

195

As fast as you can you grab the jar and scoop out a big handful of the sticky paste inside. With far less precision than last time, you throw the paste onto the painted lips. *Splat!* The gooey mess dribbles

down the picture and drips off the edge of the golden frame.
Go to 63

196

The **knitted puppet** chuckles. "So you say, so you say. Can you see the colours of a goblins scales? See what colour my skin is, eh? Tell me, what colour scales would we never see on a goblin?"
If you say black scales, go to 71
If you say brown scales, go to 449

197

If you want Adrienne to attack Clawed Dragon, go to 257
If you want Adrienne to heal herself, go to 243
If you want Adrienne to heal Kyla, go to 161
If you want Adrienne to heal you, go to 480

198

"Bah!" grumbles the **knitted puppet**. "Here's where your lucky streak ends, my colour blind nemesis! Tell me the colour of this purple sock?"
If you say purple, go to 86
If you say something else, go to 74

199

If you examine the body of the goblin, go to 83
If you look in the larder door, go to 413
If you leave by the north door, go to 451
If you leave by the south door, go to 206

200

Kyla is engulfed in a blaze.
Kyla collapses, exhausted.
Clawed Dragon beats its chest and hollers for help.
Swift Elf comes to its aid!
Go to 234

201

The moment you hand touches the lever a burst of immense electrical current surges through your hand. Unlucky for Kyla, she is stood touching you and is also court by the blast.

Melded to the spot as the energy fries through you, sparks crack and sizzle about your head.

If you have a purple glow, go to 330
Otherwise, go to 194

202

Sai howls and lashes out with beak hands.

Crack! A successful hit.

The **golden shield** is crushed to dust. Massive Elf can no longer use the **golden shield**.

Massive Elf is bleeding.

Go to 362

203

Kyla attacks Hob Goblin.

Hob Goblin successfully defends himself with the **blue shield**. Hob Goblin is unaffected.

Hob Goblin raises the **purple stick** and casts a 'DEEP BOLT' spell on Kyla.

Bang! A stunning hit.

Kyla collapses, exhausted.

You move next.
Go to 434

204

You attack Hob Goblin.

Crack! A successful hit.

The **purple stick** cracks and snaps in two. Hob Goblin can no longer use the **purple stick**.

The **icy stick** cracks and snaps in two. You can no longer use the **icy stick**.

Hob Goblin collapses, exhausted.

Hob Goblin drops **1 glittered pebble**.

You can hold up to **20 glittered pebbles** *and together they will still count as only one item. If you want to keep it, note you have gained* **1 glittered pebble.**

Go to 251

205

The cabinet's made of very thick glass. Somehow it has become steamed up and so it is hard to see what is inside. It looks like some kind of weapon is there, but it is too hard to see.

Kyla sighs and scratches her head.

You cannot get to this item at the moment.

If you leave by the north door, go to 450

If you leave by the south door, go to 431

206

The walls, floor and ceiling here are made from stretched flesh. Twitching and flexing about this skin are hundreds of fingers and single staring eyes, large, lidless, deep blue. Two of these eyes, high on the east wall, are near a thin, open mouth, drooling tongue hanging from toothless gums.

"Come to me!" the mouth hisses, and five outstretched fingers quiver in your direction.

If you take hold of the hand, go to 12

If you leave by the north archway, go to 190

If you leave by the west door, go to 431

207

The first two trunks are already open and empty. The remaining trunk is full of papers. One scroll is entitled *'The Black Goblin Myth Exposed'*. Two large books are labelled *'A Spinach Salter's Guide, parts I - VI'*. A small pamphlet covered in red ink stains is called *'Making Bombs From Bambadeen, Weapons From The Purple Poison'*. There are a number of loose pages with the words 'Tin roof, rusted' scribbled down then scribbled out again.

If you leave the red rock cavern through the west door, go to 114

If you leave the red rock cavern through the north door, go to 150

If you leave the red rock cavern through the east door, go to 206

208

No sooner are you both through the portal than you find yourselves skidding down a soft, slimy slope. You arrive with a splash in a small, shallow pool of sticky liquid. The pink walls around you look like marshmallow, but marshmallow covered with hundreds of squiggly blue lines.

"Veins!" gasps Kyla. "We're inside some sort of creature's gut!"

A deep gurgling rumbles above your heads and the pink

walls quiver.

If you have a flying carpet and want to try using it, go to 121
If you have a lucky charm and want to try using it, go to 522
If you have salted spinach and want to try using it, go to 225
If you have none of these items, go to 293

209

You are in the goblins' sleeping quarters. At the moment, it is empty. There is a small table beside a pair of wooden bunk beds and three exits leading out of this room.

If you look at the table by the bed, go to 433
If you leave by the north door, go to 217
If you leave by the west door, go to 390
If you leave by the south door, go to 475

210

You and Sai have stepped into a purple bricked torture chamber! Chains hang from the ceiling, an iron maiden lies open to one side, and two large wooden racks fill the centre of the room. There are two other exits out of here, one in the north and one in the south wall. Sai shudders.

"This used to be Lyric's favourite room. Now she has a new abuse suite up in her private tower."

A low growling snarl sounds from between the two racks. Slowly and sure footed, a massive, blue, two headed dog strides out to face you. Both its mouths drip wet with green drool.

If you run back through the west door to the elevator gargoyle room, go to 299
If you stand your ground, got to 439

211

You invoke the spirit of Ember and slice at Swift Elf with **cobra sceptre**!

Swift Elf successfully defends herself with the **golden shield**.

Swift Elf is unaffected.
Go to 394

212

"Wh- what?" Sai stares in disbelief at his cockerel and lizard hands.

"Fairy, you're brilliant!" Kyla exclaims. "Look - we're all perfectly healed! Wow! I can't believe it. I never thought I would ever see such amazing powers."

"Oh, you will see far more than this," Fairy assures her. "You have a great destiny ahead of you back in your homeland, Kyla. You are only beginning to realise your own true strengths."

"Home..." echoes Adrienne. "Fairy, can you really send us back?"

"I can't, but Kyla can. She knows the **'DEEP PORTAL'** spell. Once you have cast it, the rifts between our worlds will seal and close forever. Friends, we could never have beaten Lyric without you. Now this land will remain at peace. Thank you, our brave champions!"

"Then it really is finished," says Adrienne. "After everything that's happened. We're going home."

"Wait!"

Zuri steps forward. He wraps his arm around your waist. Adrienne and Kyla watch in disbelief.

"Don't go," Zuri presses his nose against yours. "Stay with me."

"Hey!" Adrienne grabs Zuri's shoulder. "Let go! We're leaving now. Get off!"

If you want to stay with Zuri, go to 239
If you want to return home with Kyla and Adrienne, go to 310

213

⚔ Fight!

Hob Goblin (Weapons: **purple stick / blue shield**)

Hob Goblin attacks you.

If you are carrying cobra shield, go to 121
If not, but you are carrying a purple glow, go to 357
If not, but you are carrying a blue shield, go to 92
If you have none of these, go to 227

214

You invoke the spirit of Ember and slice Duke Elf in half with **cobra sceptre**!
Duke Elf collapses, exhausted.
Duke Elf drops **purple stick**.
Duke Elf drops **golden shield**.
Duke Elf drops **10 glittered pebbles**.
Duke Elf's magical hold over Adrienne has been broken!
Adrienne picks up and equips **purple stick**.
Adrienne picks up and equips **golden shield**.
Adrienne picks up **10 glittered pebbles**.
Adrienne will now fight at your side!
Sai moves next. Go to 349

215

You are defenceless!
If you try telling the creature that you are against Lyric too, go to 381
If you attack again, go to 469

216

There's a scroll in the trunk. It reads: *'The Dream Mollusc cannot harm you when you are awake. Do not sleep! Stay awake tonight.'*
With nothing else here, you leave by the door you came in by.
Go to 209

217

"Hey, we've come to an elevator room!" cheers Kyla.
Sure enough, a circular, orange brick shaft stands directly in

front of you in the north wall. There are no other doors other than the one through which you just came. To your left is a padlocked cupboard. Beside it is a steel trunk. The entrance to the elevator is open but no elevator is inside.

"Hello?" you call up the shaft, but get no reply. You see no button or lever for the elevator.

If you look in the trunk, go to 216
If you leave by the south door, go to 209

218
Nothing happens.
If you turn the dial left, go to 5
If you turn the dial right, go to 226
If you do not turn the dial again, go to 246

219
A deep, mechanical rumbling can be heard. Then, all about you, the room begins to quake. Kyla clings to your arm, although the platform on which your standing seems to be remaining stable. With a long, groaning creak, the entire room begins to move! The ledge you're stood on appears to be the axis as the space starts to rotate! Slowly the whole place turns, until the roof becomes the wall, the wall becomes the floor, until finally everything is the right way up.
If you leave by the north door, go to 209
If you leave by the west door, go to 450
If you leave by the south door, go to 190

220
Cobra bracelet glows.

*This panel is a **slab of glittered marble** save point. Make a separate note of the items and spells you and your companions are carrying now. At any point from now on, you can return back through time to panel **220**, minus any items or spells you collect after saving your adventure here.*

"This is elevator gargoyle room of Lyric's castle," Sai states.

"We must find Ember. Let's go!"

If you look inside the entrance to the elevator, go to 299

If you jump through the small hole in the floor, go to 414

If you leave by the west door, go to 287

If you leave by the east door, go to 210

221

You invoke the spirit of Ember and slice at Mysterious Elf with **cobra sceptre**!

Mysterious Elf successfully defends himself with the **golden shield**.

Mysterious Elf is unaffected.

If you want Sai to move next, go to 192

If you want Kyla to move next, go to 521

222

Kyla raises the **purple stick** and casts a '**DEEP BOLT**' spell on Whispering Elf.

Bang! A stunning hit.

Whispering Elf collapses, exhausted.

Whispering Elf drops **6 glittered pebbles**.

If you want to keep them, note you have gained **6 glittered pebbles**.

Go to 348

223

The trunk is empty.

If you look through the window, go to 72

If you leave by the north door, go to 514

If you leave by the east door, go to 450

If you leave by the portal in the south wall, go to 208

224

"No!" Lyric staggers back, a look of amazement grasping her dying face. "You don't... you fools! You don't even know what you've done..."

The Queen elf is dead. You have won!

"You're finished, Lyric!" laughs Kyla, firing a final **'DEEP BOLT'** at the defeated monarch.

"Sai..."

You slowly approach your friends lifeless body. Adrienne comes to your side.

"Oh, god. I'm so sorry. He helped you a lot, didn't he?" she asks.

You nod.

"And with **cobra bracelet** broken, there's no way I can change time to save him."

"Oh, Sai," Kyla also joins you by the fallen magitright. "I didn't know him for long, but I know how he guided you when you thought I had died. God, how many people were killed because of that evil Queen? Who do you think will rule the land now that she is dead?"

"That's not our concern now," Adrienne replies. "We're all back together, at last. Kyla, you know the **'DEEP PORTAL'** spell, right? We should leave now, before anything else bad happens."

"Hey! We can't just leave," Kyla protests. "We've got to at least tell someone what's happened."

"Everyone's dead!" Adrienne turns to you. "Tell her. We should go while we can, shouldn't we?"

If you tell Kyla to cast 'DEEP PORTAL' now, go to 310

If you look for survivors, go to 384

225

Getting down on your knees, you start to rub the **salted spinach** into the monster's stomach. As you quicken your scrubs, it begins to wobble underneath you, then slowly begin to descend.

"It's working. It's going to chuck us up! Hold on!"

Ping! The stomach floor springs back and shoots you both upward and into the portal above.

Take the **salted spinach** *off of your list of items, as it cannot be used again.*
Go to 114

226
Nothing happens.
If you turn the dial left, go to 346
If you turn the dial right, go to 456
If you do not turn the dial again, go to 246

227
Crack! A successful hit.
You are bleeding.
If you want Kyla to move first, go to 203
If you want to move first, go to 434

228
Fairy is no bigger than your fingernail.
"Hey there!" she squeaks. "Do you have any **glittered pebbles**? I collect **glittered pebbles** to use for my spells. If you have any **glittered pebbles**, I'll gladly make an exchange!"

Jar of **salted spinach**	**1 glittered pebble**
bottle of space	**1 glittered pebble**
bottle of oil	**2 glittered pebbles**
blue shield	**2 glittered pebbles**
metal club	**3 glittered pebbles**
purple glow	**7 glittered pebbles**
cobra shield	**14 glittered pebbles**
3 gold coins	**20 glittered pebbles**

You can take as many items as you can carry (remember, you can carry up to six items and no more) as long as you have the right number of **glittered pebbles** *to make the exchange. If you can't afford an item, you can't have it! However, if you have enough* **glittered pebbles** *to buy more than one of any item, up to ten of each are* *potentially available. If you choose to make any purchases note what they are and remember to deduct the appropriate number of* **glittered pebbles**.

"Nice to do business with you," squeaks Fairy. "See you again!"
Go to 399

229
If you have cobra sceptre, go to 121
If not, but you have a metal club, go to 87
If not, but you have an icy stick, go to 232
If you have none of these, go to 524

230
✒ Fight!
Dribbling Goblin (Weapons: **icy stick / blue shield**)
Muttering Goblin (Weapons: **purple stick / blue shield**)

Dribbling Goblin attacks Sai.
Sai giggles and skips out of range.
Sai is unaffected.
If you want Sai to move first:
If you want Sai to attack Dribbling Goblin, go to 4
If you want Sai to attack Muttering Goblin, go to 104
If you want to move first:
If you attack Dribbling Goblin, go to 440
If you attack Muttering Goblin, go to 273

231
Sai will now accompany you on your travels through the castle. As Sai does not have hands, he is not able to carry anything, so unfortunately the maximum number of items you can carry is still six. He will, however, act as your advisor and be yours to command in battle.

You sit down to tell Sai your long, sad story, of how Adrienne's ritual reacted with Filth's pentagram, how the Queen elf kidnapped Adrienne, how Hob goblin murdered Kyla, everything. Sai listens solemnly, never interrupting, occasionally shivering in anger as he hears yet more of Lyric's recent cruelty. You've not quite completed your tale when the sound of the elevator alerts you both.

"Goblins! This time it really is. Brace yourself for attack."

The magitright is right. As the granite platform raises to castle level two green scaled soldiers tumble out, weapons raised, ready to slay some rebels!

Go to 230

232

You attack Hob Goblin.

Crack! A successful hit.

The **blue shield** cracks and snaps in two. Hob Goblin can no longer use the **blue shield**.

Hob Goblin is bleeding.

Hob Goblin raises the **purple stick** and casts a 'DEEP BOLT' spell on you.

Bang! A stunning hit.

You are bleeding.

If you want Kyla to move next, go to 140

If you want to move next, go to 49

233

Kyla raises the **purple stick** and casts a 'DEEP INFERNO' spell on Duke Elf, Mysterious Elf, Clawed Dragon and Lyric.

Smash! An outstanding hit.

Duke Elf is bleeding.

Smash! An outstanding hit.

Mysterious Elf collapses, exhausted.

Mysterious Elf drops **8 glittered pebbles**.

If you want to keep them, note you have gained **8 glittered pebbles**.

Clawed Dragon is out of range.

Clawed Dragon is unaffected.

Lyric is out of range.

Lyric is unaffected.

Duke Elf beats his chest and hollers for help.

Massive Elf comes to his aid!

Massive Elf attacks Sai.

Sai giggles and skips out of range.

Sai is unaffected.

If you want Sai to move next, go to 133

If you move next, go to 314

234

Swift Elf raises the **purple stick** and casts a '**DEEP INFERNO**' spell on you, Sai and Adrienne.

Smash! An outstanding hit.

Sai collapses, exhausted.

Smash! An outstanding hit.

Adrienne collapses, exhausted.

Smash! An outstanding hit.

Cobra shield implodes in thick yellow gas. You can no longer use **cobra shield**.

You are bleeding.

Clawed Dragon swoops!

Clawed Dragon spews a ball of fire at you.

You are engulfed in a blaze.

The **purple** glow implodes in thick yellow gas. You can no longer use the **purple glow**.

You collapse, exhausted.

Clawed Dragon soars up and out of range.

Go to 432

235

Armoured Skeletal Knight attacks you.

Crack! A successful hit.

You collapse, exhausted.

Go to 313

236

"Who's there? Answer me!"

There is no reply.

Go to 167

237

There are three wooden framed doorways set into the rock face around you. In the corner are three large steel trunks. All are open and contain nothing of further use.

If you leave the red rock cavern through the west door, go to 315

If you leave the red rock cavern through the north door, go to 15

If you leave the red rock cavern through the east door, go to 482

238

"I just came up from the dungeon. I was stupid and fell asleep. Luckily I knew to attack the red head. You don't know what I mean? Well, I wasn't asleep long enough to ask its name!"

Go to 399

239

"I'm not going back," you tell them. "Zuri told me I would fall in love with this land. I want to stay here."

"What?" Adrienne looks like she's about to punch the young elf. "What about us?"

"I understand," says Kyla, softly. "I feel torn, too. I have to go back though. I have no choice."

"Come on, Fairy," whispers Sai. "I think we should leave them to it."

"This is crazy!" splutters Adrienne. "Look, there's only one **'DEEP PORTAL'** spell, right? Not using it with us is mad! Come on, you're making such a mistake. Pull yourself together."

"No," says Zuri, calmly. "We're staying here. Accept it."

"You could come with us, Zuri?" offers Kyla, but he shakes

his head.

"If you feel as strongly about your world as I do my homeland, you will understand."

"You two could stay here with us," you suggest.

"What?" Adrienne nearly explodes at this idea. "No! How can you do this to me? To Kyla? I thought we were in love?"

"I'll look after her," Kyla assures you. "I'm going to miss you so much, but I get why you're doing this. I love you." She throws her arms around you and squeezes you tight.

"Adrienne?" You look over but she has turned her back upon you. "Let's say goodbye."

"I have nothing else to say. Kyla, take us home."

Kyla nods, raises the **purple stick**. "Don't be angry with Adrienne," she sighs. "She'll get it in time. God, I'm really going to miss you. Are you sure you don't want to come back?"

You look at Zuri then shake your head. Kyla nods, casts the **'DEEP PORTAL'** spell and with a small flash of light, she and Adrienne are gone.

Go to 172

240

"It is true, my spells are not strong enough to cure my own wounds. I can use my remaining strength to ensure you, Kyla and Sai are at full power for the final fight. May I please heal you now?"

If you say 'yes', go to 418
If you say 'no', if you now talk to Fairy instead, go to 60
If you talk to Sai, go to 270
If you return to the elevator gargoyle, go to 519

241

Sai howls and lashes out with beak hands.

Crack! A successful hit.

The **golden shield** is crushed to dust. Mysterious Elf can no longer use the **golden shield**.

Mysterious Elf is bleeding.

Go to 362

242

Sai howls and lashes out with beak hands.

Sai misses!

Handsome Elf is unaffected.

Go to 509

243

Adrienne raises the **purple stick** and casts a '**DEEP HEAL**' spell on herself.

Adrienne is fine.

Go to 316

244

You and Sai step into a small room which has two other exits, one in its west and one in its south wall.

Sure enough, the hell hound is here, along with a pair of its double-headed brothers!

Go to 258

245

Kyla raises the **purple stick** and casts a '**DEEP INFERNO**' spell on Lyric.

Smash! An outstanding hit.

The **golden shield** is crushed to dust. Lyric can no longer use the **golden shield**.

Lyric is bleeding.

Go to 496

246

If you have a tin box and want to look at it, go to 499

If not, you can leave this hut by its east exit, go to 253

Or, if you leave by the south exit, if you then look about the south-most hut, go to 73

If you then look about the west-most hut, go to 463

If you return through the gates into the castle, go to 299

247

"Kyla!"

From the shadows runs forward the love you thought dead. She flings herself into your arms.

"Adrienne's alive!" she gasps. "Ember told me. He saved me from death. He is amazing!"

"But what if we just want to go home?" you ask the wizard. "Take Kyla and Adrienne and leave?"

"Then let it be. Our land will fall. Slavery and torture will await our people. But I cannot force you to stay. I have gifted Kyla the single use of a **'DEEP PORTAL'** spell. Use it at any time to go back home, though be aware if Adrienne is not with you, the spell will only carry the two of you."

At any one time you can ask Kyla to cast **'DEEP PORTAL'.** *When you wish to do so, go to* **527.**

"Let your conscience guide you, friends," Ember advises. "My time is spent. I have sustained my spirit's projection as long as I can. At last, I die. Go find **cobra sceptre**. You are our final hope..."

Ember's image flickers and fades. The light is gone. All is darkness again.

Go to 186

248

Fairy flutters her wings and casts a **'DEEP HEAL'** spell on Sai. Sai is fine.

Fairy flutters her wings and casts a **'DEEP HEAL'** spell on

Kyla.

Kyla is fine.

Fairy flutters her wings and casts a **'DEEP HEAL'** spell on Adrienne.

Adrienne is fine.

Fairy flutters her wings and casts a **'DEEP HEAL'** spell on you.

You are fine.

Go to 212

249

"You defeated dream mollusc. As I knew you would."

The light fades from the slug's battered body. A new glow radiates. It comes from a tall, uncoiled, upright snake, watching you with cool, lidless eyes, towering up at least twice your height.

"Brave one! My name is Ember. Lyric killed my mortal form and has tried to keep my spirit from linking into the realm of life. Her wizards constructed dream mollusc to imprison me. From this point, between realities, I sensed the aura of you and your companions. It was no accident you came here."

"It was you? Then Kyla is dead because of you! You're no better than Lyric."

Ember sighs. "I planted ideas of magic in Adrienne's dreams to speed up proceedings, though you would have eventually discovered on your own that your strengths are way beyond those of ordinary mortals'. My spells cannot deliver my own spirit back to the realm of life, but I have had the soul of Kyla saved here, ready to fulfil both your destinies."

You shake your head. This is all too much. Magic? Destiny? "No. I'm just like anyone else."

"Not true. You have witnessed but a fraction of the powers you will accomplish. Your place is as legend, in both our world and yours. Only you will wield **cobra sceptre**, a unique blade with the strength to cut even a dragon's skin. I have it hidden in the dungeon, away from Lyric's elite guard. I am asking you to

retrieve **cobra sceptre**, and with it destroy Lyric for good!"
Go to 247

250

Sai howls and lashes out with beak hands.

Crack! A successful hit.

Muttering Goblin collapses, exhausted.

Muttering Goblin drops **3 glittered pebbles**.

You can hold up to **20 glittered pebbles** *and together they will still count as only one item. If you want to keep them, note you have gained* **3 glittered pebbles**.

You move next.

You attack Dribbling Goblin, go to 152

251

"Ugh!"

Hob goblin writhes on the floor clutching his chest. From the chinks in his red armour, thick green blood oozes out into pools about his body.

"Your first kill..?" he manages a weak grin. "How does it feel? I hope it makes you feel... good..."

Hob goblin dies.

"A... Adrienne?" Crushed against the side of the elevator chute, Kyla sits, stony eyed. You rush to her, call her name, put your hands above her head. She is not breathing. Opening her mouth, pinching shut her nose, you desperately force your own exhausted breath into your lover's lungs. You breathe. You breathe.

"Kyla!" you shout at her body, "Kyla, come on!"

Everything is still. The only noise in the dungeon is your own ragged breath. Kyla is dead.

Go to 105

252

Smash! An outstanding hit.

Sai is bleeding.

Smash! An outstanding hit.

Kyla is bleeding.

Cobra shield flickers and the spirit of Ember wraps around your body!

You are unaffected.

Go to 126

253

This is the village square. Two old goat men are looking seriously up at an rock statue of a proud King. Fairy's hut is to the west. There is another hut to the east.

If you speak to the first goat man, go to 484

If you speak to the second goat man, go to 367

If you look about the west-most hut, go to 116

If you look about the east-most hut, go to 506

254

If you want Adrienne to attack Lyric, go to 7

If you want Adrienne to heal herself, go to 373

If you want Adrienne to heal Kyla, go to 483

If you want Adrienne to heal you, go to 283

255

Rock Troll attacks you.

Bang! A stunning hit.

You collapse, exhausted.

Go to 370

256

You invoke the spirit of Ember and slice at Clawed Dragon with **cobra sceptre**!

You miss!

Clawed Dragon is unaffected.

Go to 316

257

Adrienne attacks Clawed Dragon.

Adrienne misses!

Clawed Dragon is unaffected.

Go to 316

258

⚔ Fight!

Hell Hound	(Weapons: none)
Hell Hound	(Weapons: none)
Hell Hound	(Weapons: none)

Hell Hound attacks Sai.

Sai giggles and skips out of range.

Sai is unaffected.

Hell Hound attacks Sai.

Crack! A successful hit.

Sai collapses, exhausted.

Hell Hound attacks you.

If you have cobra shield, go to 121

If not, but you have purple glow, go to 490

If you have neither of these items, go to 513

259

"Please, let me rest," he asks without looking up. "I will see you once Alchemist has been."

Sai advises you let the elf have some time on his own.

If you look about the west-most hut, go to 463

If you look about the north-most hut, go to 116

If you return through the gates into the castle, go to 299

260

You act without thinking. You pull out the **bone**, brandish it like a sword in front of you. Sai freezes, watching from a safer distance thinking you've gone mad. The skeleton freezes too, examining the **bone** silently. Slowly, it reaches out its hand, and you gently place the **bone** into its palm. Only now do you notice that the hand it held out has one finger missing. Giving a wary nod of thanks, the ghoul takes small backwards steps toward the hole it created, and carefully climbs back inside.

*Make sure you now deduct the **bone** from your items list.*

"I thought we were gonnas!" chuckles Sai. "Got any more tricks like that up your sleeve?"

Your foe now departed, together you march boldly up to the gate and make your way inside. As you pass under the portcullis it lowers with a loud rattle behind you, blocking your way back out.

Go to 68

261

Now that Kyla is no longer with you, your maximum number of items you can take is limited to no more than six. If, between you, you already had more than six items, you must choose which you are to leave behind here and which you are to keep. If in future you find an item you could potentially take but you already have six items, you must select an existing item to discard if you want to take the new one. Bare in mind though that you do not usually have to take every item that's available.

"Woe... woe is me!"

Who said that? A faint trundling sound from the shaft catches your ear. In the shaft before you descends the elevator gargoyle, a thick 'L' shaped platform made of solid granite with a small, squashed face in the centre of its back wall.

"Oh no. You'll be another one wanting to use me, then. That's all anybody does, use me. I may as well have 'use me' engraved on my forehead."

"Er... you do," you tell the gargoyle.

"Oh do I? I didn't know that!" comes the sarcastic reply.

"Let's get it over with then. Climb aboard."
If you step onto the elevator gargoyle, go to 54
If you open the steel chest first, go to 462

262

Sai howls and lashes out with beak hands.
Sai misses!
Armoured Skeletal Knight is unaffected.
Go to 235

263

You invoke the spirit of Ember and slice at Clawed Dragon
with **cobra sceptre**!
A small chunk of scaled armour falls from Clawed Dragon's
belly.
Clawed Dragon is bleeding.
Lyric leaps down from Clawed Dragon's back.
Clawed Dragon spews a ball of fire at you.
You are engulfed in a blaze.
The **purple glow** implodes in thick yellow gas. You can no
longer use the **purple glow**.
You are bleeding.
Kyla raises the **purple stick** and casts a '**DEEP INFERNO**' spell
on Clawed Dragon and Lyric.
Smash! An outstanding hit.
Clawed Dragon collapses, exhausted.
Lyric is out of range.
Lyric is unaffected.
Go to 498

264

You brandish the **purple glow** and wrap Mollusc Head in a
distorted aura.
Crack! A successful hit.

Mollusc Head moans.

Mollusc Head beats his chest and hollers for help.

Nothing happens.

With a slurping groan, neon Mollusc Head exchanges places with the head in front of it.

Mollusc Head growls and bubbles slime.

Mollusc Head inhales.

If you attack the closest Mollusc Head, go to 459

If you attack the middle Mollusc Head, go to 335

If you attack the furthest Mollusc Head, go to 396

265

If you want Adrienne to attack Lyric, go to 7

If you want Adrienne to heal herself, go to 373

If you want Adrienne to heal Sai, go to 419

If you want Adrienne to heal you, go to 317

266

The **silver ring** reflects light into his eyes. He looks up and for the first time he sees your face.

"That's a handsome piece of jewellery you've got there." He smiles warmly and leans back in his chair. "Like its owner. Did your lover get you that?"

"Zuri, stop flirting!" tuts Sai dismissively. "We've no time for that now."

The elf ignores him, continues to smile. "You know, I would love you to have dinner with me. You're not too busy to eat, are you? Sorry, Sai, only enough for two."

If you say you will eat with the elf, go to 281

If you explain about Adrienne and your search for Ember, go to 474

267

Sai howls and lashes out with beak hands.

Bang! A stunning hit.

Clawed Dragon collapses, exhausted.
Go to 430

268

You are bathed in foggy light from the **purple glow**.
You are unaffected.
If you want Kyla to attack the Fat Elf, go to 146
If you attack the Fat Elf, go to 296

269

Adrienne raises the **purple stick** and casts a **'DEEP HEAL'** spell on Sai.
Sai is fine.
Go to 523

270

"Your confidence is misplaced," Sai wheezes. "We have lost."
If you talk to Freja the goblin, go to 240
If you talk to Fairy, go to 60
If you return to the elevator gargoyle, go to 519

271

"We've been moving our headquarters around the castle so that it is harder for Lyric to find us," she reports. "When Sai did not return to us, we thought he had been defeated. Sai is the greatest warrior in the Rebellion. He is so tough he doesn't even need to use weapons or shields!"
Go to 399

272

Uncorking the **bottle of space** with your teeth, you lob the entire contents over the evil ghoul. As the white liquid hits its body, the skeleton emits a high pitched shriek, smoulders and burns. In moments, the once massive creature of darkness is no more than ash on a tombstone.

"Hey!" chuckles Sai. "I thought we were gonnas! Got any more tricks like that up your sleeve?"

Deduct **bottle of space** *from your items list.*

Your foe defeated, together you march through the castle gate. As you pass under the portcullis it lowers with a loud rattle, blocking the way back out.

Go to 68

273

You attack Muttering Goblin.

Crack! A successful hit.

The **blue shield** cracks and snaps in two. Muttering Goblin can no longer use the **blue shield**.

Muttering Goblin is bleeding.

Muttering Goblin raises the **purple stick** and casts a '**DEEP HEAL**' spell on himself.

Muttering Goblin is fine.

Go to 502

274

Adrienne raises the **purple stick** and casts a '**DEEP HEAL**' spell on Kyla.

Kyla is fine.

Go to 158

275

Thinking quick, you blow hard on the **silver whistle**. Then you blow again, as no noise seems to have come out. Desperate, you blow a third time. Then you realise that Sai is laughing.

"It's working! Look!"

The hell hound is jerking its head left and right, trying but unable to locate the source of the noise, sounding at a frequency too high for your ears to register but evidentially distressing to the beast. With a pathetic yap from its right-hand head, it scampers away through the south wall door.

"Ha!" chuckles Sai. "I thought we were gonnas! Got any more tricks like that up your sleeve?"

You take another look at the **silver whistle**. You blew so hard upon it, it has come apart around the mouth piece.

Discard the **silver whistle** *from your item list as it will not work again.*

"There's no stopping us now. Let's go!"

If you leave by the north door, go to 65

If you leave by the west door, go to 299

If you leave by the south door, go to 244

276

You and Sai bid Zuri farewell and then make your way from his home.

"Don't mind Zuri," Sai shrugs as you cross the village. "He just wears his heart on his sleeve. He has been an invaluable member of the Rebellion since Lyric started talking about war."

If you look about the west-most hut, go to 463
If you look about the north-most hut, go to 116
If you return through the gates into the castle, go to 299

277

The hell hound lunges, pinning you to the floor. Sai is yelling something you can't make out. Two hundred pounds of hairy fat crushes against you as the first head rips into your shoulder, tearing through tendons. Blood flies. The second head presses against yours, its nose hot and dry. Jaws open. They smell like honey. Then they clamp around your neck.

Go to 194

278

Smash! An outstanding hit.

Sai is bleeding.

You are bathed in foggy light from the **purple glow**.

You are unaffected.

If you want Sai to attack Handsome Elf, go to 59
If you attack Handsome Elf, go to 371

279

Kyla raises the **purple stick** and casts a '**DEEP INFERNO**' spell on Clawed Dragon and Lyric.

Clawed Dragon is out of range.

Clawed Dragon is unaffected.

Lyric is out of range.

Lyric is unaffected.

Go to 316

280

Cloaked Elf beats her chest and hollers for help.

Sniggering Elf comes to her aid!

Sniggering Elf attacks Kyla.

Crack! A successful hit.

Kyla is bleeding.

Whispering Elf attacks you.

Crack! A successful hit.

You collapse, exhausted.

Go to 446

281

Sai lets out a long breath and rolls his eyes.

"Well, since we're in the village I should try to gather support for the Rebellion. I guess you're staying here with Zuri for a bit." Shaking his head, he leaves.

Zuri chuckles and gets to his feet.

"Sai is such an old man. We've both been part of the Rebellion ever since Lyric killed the King. I bust my arm up fighting one of Lyric's elite guard. Soon as Alchemist has me cured I'll be back in action."

He gives you a wink and bends down by a low cupboard. Together you prepare a steaming hot vegetable stew over an open fire round the back of his hut. Effortlessly, you talk about the paths you've both taken to get here. He tells you about his people and home. You tell him about your life and the trials you've faced so far. Becoming tearful when speaking of Adrienne and Kyla, Zuri gently wraps an arm around your shoulder. Once dinner is ready you both sit down on the earthy hut floor to eat.

"Zuri! We know you're there," a guttural voice snarls from outside. "Come out and fight, rebel!"

"We're trapped," Zuri curses, punching his fist on his knee. "We have no choice but to attack."

Go to 113

282

"Ding dong! Off you go," the elevator gargoyle groans.

He chucks you out and into a room identical to the one you just left, except this one's walls are a light green and there are only two other exits. The one in the west wall is significantly bigger than the one opposite it in the east. There is a small hole in the floor. Next to a large steel trunk a hunched figure is sat with its back to you, breathing heavily.

"Leave me, like everyone does," sobs the elevator gargoyle, and with that he is gone.

"What? More goblins?"

The unknown figure jumps to its feet and spins round to face you. It is a creature wearing thick, bronze armour, its face hairy and whiskered, its large, round eyes a glittering gold. Its ears look like a wolf's, and instead of hands two other heads end its very long arms. On its right arm is what looks like the head of a large cockerel, whilst the left is a beaked lizard.

"Scum of Lyric!" spits the beast. "I am not your slave! I attack for all magitrights. For the Rebellion!"

Go to 441

283

Adrienne raises the **purple stick** and casts a '**DEEP HEAL**' spell on you.

You are fine.

If you want Kyla to attack Lyric, go to 427

If you attack Lyric, go to 110

284

"Ha! Alchemist's hut. Hello, sir!" greets Sai, waving his cockerel arm at the slim man inside the small building.

Dressed in long blue and white robes, Alchemist is holding a large number of papers and scrolls. He looks quite stressed as he dithers backward and forward.

"Oh, yes, Sai. Lovely as always. I am rather behind with visits today. So many have been injured in skirmishes with the elite guard, yet still the people will not believe Lyric is preparing for war. Oh my, you two look like you've been in a scrape. Here, let me see to your wounds."

Alchemist finds a large jar labelled *'red lum'* and massages some of the red paste into your scars.

"Remarkable stuff!" comments Alchemist. "Good for insomnia too. Get the red to see you safe through a good night's sleep, they say. Now, who's next? Ah, off to Zuri! Where did I put his files?"

You and Sai are now both at full health.

If you leave by the hut's west door, go to 253
If you leave by the hut's east door, go to 177

285

You attack Dribbling Goblin.

Crack! A successful hit.

Dribbling Goblin is bleeding.

Muttering Goblin raises the **purple stick** and casts a **'DEEP HEAL'** spell on Dribbling Goblin.

Dribbling Goblin is fine.

Go to 502

286

You attack Hell Hound.

Crack! A successful hit.

Hell Hound is bleeding.

Go to 503

287

"Sai... it's beautiful. Is it real... or just more sorcery?"

A sunlit meadow surrounds you. Beyond that, a pastoral landscape of light woods and yellow fields fill the horizon. A soft, heathery scent tickles your nose. A small cluster of thatched straw huts are grouped together beside some great oak trees. South of them is a patch of corn, just ready to be harvested. To the north, on your right, is a small, shallow lake, a family of duck billed birds going about their own business back and to from the leafy bank. The gentle waves of the lake, caused by a slight breeze in the air, lap against the giant, grey walls of the castle you have just left.

"This is real," smiles Sai. "We're outside Lyric's castle. No witchcraft here, just the good village folk going about their daily work. These people will be the first to be enslaved should the planned war go ahead. They refuse to believe the true terror their murderous new Queen is preparing."

If you look about the south-most hut, go to 73
If you look about the west-most hut, go to 463
If you look about the north-most hut, go to 116
If you return through the gates into the castle, go to 299

288

"With Ember gone, I am the new leader of the Rebellion," says the elf. "Dragon Claw Keep used to be ruled by our beloved King, until Lyric murdered our monarch and made herself Queen of Dorho. Now she has this castle she plans to wage war against the rest of the land with her goblin army. We've been planning an attack on her private tower, but many of our numbers have already been killed or wounded by Lyric's elite guard. But now we have a healer in our ranks I am hoping we will soon be powerful enough to take her by surprise."

Go to 399

289

You attack Dribbling Goblin.
Crack! A successful hit.
Dribbling Goblin is bleeding.
Muttering Goblin raises the **purple stick** and casts a '**DEEP**

HEAL' spell on Dribbling Goblin.

Dribbling Goblin is fine.

Dribbling Goblin attacks you.

Crack! A successful hit.

You collapse, exhausted.

Go to 181

290

✒ Fight!

Bubble   (Weapons: none)

If you have any new weapons / shields you may equip them here.

If you want Kyla to move first, go to 460

If you want to move first, go to 165

291

"I'm going to stay here and catch up with the Rebellion," says Sai, "I'll see you in a bit."

"Woe... woe is me!" moans the elevator gargoyle as you step onto her granite platform. "That southern elevator thinks he has it so bad, if he knew half my torment! Woe, woe, woe! Here is where I'm meant to say 'I'm going down', which is ironic." She pauses. "Because I am so down."

"Yes, I got it," you reply.

"Ding dong! Off you go," she chucks you out and into an orange brick room with a single door in the south wall. To your right is a padlocked cupboard. Beside it is a steel trunk.

If you look in the trunk, go to 468

If you leave by the south door, go to 300

If you take the elevator gargoyle back up a level, go to 399

292

"Hi!" Zuri's face lights up upon seeing you. "I'm still waiting for

Alchemist, y'know. Where can he be?"
Go to 120

293

A burst of boiling stomach acid cascades down. Kyla screams as the liquid slaps her skin. The pink walls contract and the muscles of this giant creature's stomach cave in on you. In a monster this big, you must make a pretty tiny meal.
Go to 194

294

"We'd best not stay put too long," Sai warns you. "I don't think Lyric saw your arrival as any more than an amusing accident, but now the goblins she intended for war are falling. You are a threat."

"What is this war I keep hearing of?"

"No time to explain. Filth was right, you need to find Ember. You spotted these trunks scattered about the place?" Sai pats his lizard head on the one he is beside. "Let's crack open this one."

You open the trunk. Inside are a **slab of glittered marble** and a small item of jewellery.

"The **cobra bracelet**!" cheers Sai. "Oh, Lyric will be mad when she finds out we've got this."

You slide on **cobra bracelet**. It tingles on your flesh. It has fused itself onto your skin!

As **cobra bracelet** *fits on your wrist you can take it as well as the other six items you may carry. However, you cannot discard it unless it breaks.*

"Don't worry," Sai assures you, "**Cobra bracelet** is blessed."

If you still have a **compass***, discard it now.* **Cobra bracelet** *will give you a magic sense of navigation.*

"With **cobra bracelet**, you can travel short distances in time!" reveals Sai. "The **cobra bracelet** glows when you find a **slab of glittered marble**. You can then use **cobra bracelet** at any time and it'll take you back to the moment that you found the **slab of**

glittered marble. It will then be that all events which occured after passing that **slab of glittered marble** did not happen."

This means you lose items and spells found since passing that **slab of glittered marble**, *as you can't take them back in time. You will however, have all the items you had before that point, including any you've discarded or broken since then.*

Go to 220

295

"Zuri, are you all right?"

He is doubled over, the bandage torn from his arm. He grits his teeth.

"Yeah. Help me back to my hut."

You tend his wounds as best you can. Whilst you apply the dressing he stares up at the sky.

"Before Lyric, in the days of our King, this land was at peace. If we... *when* we stop her, when the Rebellion have won, I would like to show you the beauties of this land. The magic. The wonder. When this battle is over, I promise you... you'll love this land as much as I do."

You take his hand. He leans forward. You close your eyes. Your lips meet.

"I heard the sounds of battle!" Sai gasps as he rushes to the hut's doorway. "Are you both safe?"

"Just." Zuri's focus never leaves your eyes. "Take this." He gives you a **gold ring**. There are twelve planets and twenty six stars engraved deeply in it. "When I am healed I will join you in the fight. I promise you, it won't be long. Until then..."

The **gold ring** *fits around your finger so you can take it in addition to the other six items you can carry. Make a note that you now have the* **gold ring**.

Go to 276

296

You brandish the **purple glow** and wrap Fat Elf in a distorted aura.

Bang! A stunning hit.

Fat Elf's **purple glow** implodes in thick yellow gas. Fat Elf can no longer use the **purple glow**.

Kyla raises the **purple stick** and casts a '**DEEP BOLT**' spell on Fat Elf.

Bang! A stunning hit.

Fat Elf collapses, exhausted.

Fat Elf drops **5 glittered pebbles**.

If you want to keep them, note you have gained **5 glittered pebbles**.

Whispering Elf reappears.

Whispering Elf raises the **purple stick** and casts a '**DEEP BOLT**' spell on you.

You are bathed in foggy light from the **purple glow**.

You are unaffected.

If you want Kyla to attack Whispering Elf, go to 222
If you attack Whispering Elf, go to 429

297

Bang! A stunning hit.

You collapse, exhausted.

Go to 517

298

The handle on the door is stiff. You are unable to turn it.

"Oh, don't go out that way," warns Fairy. "You'll bump into Cerberus! Stay here with us!"

If you listen to her and stay, go to 399
If you decide to take this way out anyway, go to 244

299

There is nothing in here. You see no button or lever to summon the elevator.

If you jump through the small hole in the floor, go to 414

If you leave by the west door, go to 287

If you leave by the east door, go to 210

300

The door is locked. You cannot travel further into the dungeon this way just yet.

If you look in the trunk, go to 468

If you take the elevator gargoyle back up a level, go to 399

301

"Oh my word," gulps Kyla. "Smoke!"

The mouth is now actually smouldering, the reaction of the mixture causing an intense heat. A tiny flicker of fire sparks up in the corner of the lips.

"You... you savage!" cries the broken painted lady. "You will pay for this. You will die!"

If you hurry out the north door, go to 450

If you escape through the south door, go to 431

If you stand and face the broken painted lady's anger, go to 18

302

You invoke the spirit of Ember and slice Hob Goblin in half with **cobra sceptre**!

Hob Goblin collapses, exhausted.

Hob Goblin drops **2 glittered pebbles**.

If you want to keep them, note you have gained **2 glittered pebbles**.

Go to 352

303

You invoke the spirit of Ember and slice at Lyric with **cobra sceptre**!

Smash! An outstanding hit!

The **golden shield** is crushed to dust. Lyric can no longer use the **golden shield**.

Lyric is bleeding.

Go to 403

304

"Hey," calls burst bubble to the goat girl, "you've an ice compartment there for cooling hot metals?"

Goat girl nods. Burst bubble addresses Kyla and you.

"Put me in the goat girl's ice compartment and I will become an **icy stick**. Once I am frozen, I will no longer be able to talk to you, but I will be a useful weapon in battle when Lyric's minions try to stop you reaching Ember. If I break, I will die, but I would rather die in battle than remain Lyric's slave."

You pass the **wooden bucket** over to the goat girl, who places it into the ice. A few moments later your new weapon is born.

*Deduct the **wooden bucket** from your list of items and replace it with an **icy stick**. Note: You can use the **icy stick**, however Kyla is too* weak to carry this item yet, as she is still wounded from her earlier encounter with Lyric.

"Bubble is so brave," ponders Kyla. "What a sacrifice to make."

If you leave by the north door, go to 514

If you leave by the east door, go to 450

If you leave by the portal in the south wall, go to 208

305

Inside are a great number of tins and bottles of powders and pastes, many with damp or peeling labels describing their contents in an unknown text. One box contains nothing but glass tubes full of green eyeballs. Another contains a rolled up piece of parchment, *'Recipe For Blue Leaf Cake'*. A big cardboard carton contains a dozen jars of extra **salted spinach**.

If you want, you can take one jar or more of extra **salted spinach** *with you, however remember you and Kyla can only carry a maximum of six items each. Each jar counts as one item. If you decide to take any* **salted spinach**, *note how many you take on your item lists.*

Nothing else inside worth investigating, you close the larder door.

Go to 167

306

"Bah!" grumbles the **knitted puppet**. "Here's where your lucky streak ends, my colour blind nemesis! Tell me the colour of this purple sock?"

If you say purple, go to 77

If you say something else, go to 415

307

You invoke the spirit of Ember and slice Brigadier Elf in half with **cobra sceptre**!

Brigadier Elf collapses, exhausted.

Brigadier Elf drops **3 glittered pebbles**.

If you want to keep them, note you have gained **3 glittered pebbles**.
If you open the trunk, go to 223
If you look through the window, go to 72
If you leave by the north door, go to 514
If you leave by the east door, go to 450
If you leave by the portal in the south wall, go to 208

308

"Hush, hush! Show some respect!" huffles the white bearded man. "Dare you speak idle chatter in the presence of such a masterpiece as my broken painted lady."

"I'm sorry," you apologise, "but Kyla here is badly hurt."

"We were attacked by Lyric," Kyla explains. "She took Adrienne and-"

"Our Queen? Harrumph! I'm sure you whipper-snappers deserved everything you got, if you pestered her highness with the same disgraceful conduct as that with which you pester me now. Put some red lum paste on your wounds, girl, you'll be fine. Our Queen was my inspiration when composing our broken painted lady. It is my artistic expression of how every tiny aspect of her is more beauteous than the next. Each stoke painted with the finest crushed petals of the greenest tertreiah flower. I tried to near that wonder the stained glass my father created, but I don't think I did capture her splendour in quite the same magnificent way. Oh, my artistic soul is so tortured by the responsibility of my talent. Tell me, have my hours of suffering paid off? My broken painted lady, is she... is she any good?"

If you say she is good, go to 454
If you say she isn't good, go to 30
If you clout the artist for his rudeness towards you, go to 119
If you leave the artist be to look at the glass cabinet, go to 147
If you look at the plaque, go to 88
If you leave by the north door, go to 450
If you leave by the south door, through which you came, go to 431

309

Cackling Goblin attacks you.

Bang! A stunning hit.

You collapse, exhausted.

Go to 370

310

Kyla raises the **purple stick** and casts a '**DEEP PORTAL**' spell on you, Adrienne and her.

Everything starts to blur.

"Kyla?"

Nothing.

"Kyla! Are you all right?"

Rain beats harder than ever against the window of Kyla's and Adrienne's flat. Kyla is slumped on the floor, head resting on the table between Adrienne's dead candles. You gently shake her shoulder and she wakes with a start. She looks round wildly, as if she's never seen her own flat before.

"No! Lyric?"

"We're all right," Adrienne soothes her. "Everything is all right now. We're home."

Everything is as you left it. The settee, littered with papers, the results of Adrienne and you trying to guess the lyrics to 'Love Shack', what feels like a hundred lifetimes ago. The same mounds of clothes and stuffed toys all about the floor. Three cold mugs of tea on top of the telly.

"Home..." You rub your palm against your forehead. "Never thought I'd be so happy to see rain!"

"It's not over," Kyla slowly stands. "Remember what Ember told us? This is just the beginning."

"I don't believe that," Adrienne shakes her head. "I'm through with magic now. Finished."

Kyla smiles and turns away from you both. Holding up her

purple stick, she casts a '**DEEP BOLT**' spell in the air above the television. You and Adrienne flinch back from the sudden burst of heat. Kyla calmly walks over to the three hot mugs of tea, picks them up and turns back around.

"Anyone for a brew?"

311

Kyla attacks Queen Elf.

Queen Elf successfully defends herself with the **golden shield**.

Queen Elf is unaffected.

Queen Elf attacks you.

Crack! A successful hit.

You are bleeding.

Go to 98

312

Zuri rushes forward.

Zuri bellows a mighty battle cry and drives **Roxcalibur** through Lyric's heart!

Silence.

Then Lyric emits a piercing scream and dazzling light fills the room.

Lyric collapses, exhausted.

Go to 160

313

The zombie's strength is too much for either of you, and you are easily overwhelmed by your oppressor. With a lipless grin, the knight closes in for the kill.

"Use **cobra bracelet**!" splutters Sai, blood pouring from his forehead. "Go back in time, we can plan our path more carefully. We have to get better equipped. Quick, before it's too late!"

Go to 194

314
If you attack Massive Elf, go to 128
If you attack Duke Elf, go to 214

315
You and Kyla step through the west door and enter a square room with marble walls. A small chandelier hangs from the centre of the ceiling, giving almost blinding light compared to the red rock cavern you have just come from. There is one other exit in the room's north wall, a pine wood door with a gold handle. There are two large steel trunks either side of it. Along the west and south walls are giant, floor to ceiling glass cabinets. They contain row upon row of severed men's heads. Bearded, bald, young, old - the collection is huge. All have their eyes shut. In the middle of the room is a figure in long, blue robes, sat by a marble table on which are several playing cards. He is scratching his left shoulder with his left hand. The man has no head.
If you approach the headless figure, go to 171
If you try to sneak passed toward the north door, go to 426
If you go back through the east door, through which you just came, go to 237

316
  Clawed Dragon swoops!
  Clawed Dragon spews a ball of fire at you.
  Clawed Dragon misses!
  You are unaffected.
  Lyric leaps down from Clawed Dragon's back.
Go to 159

317
  Adrienne raises the **purple stick** and casts a '**DEEP HEAL**' spell on you.
  You are fine.

If you want Sai to attack Lyric, go to 417
If you attack Lyric, go to 51

318

You brandish the **purple glow** and wrap Rabid Goblin in a distorted aura.

Bang! A stunning hit.

The **blue shield** is crushed to dust. Rabid Goblin can no longer use the **blue shield**.

Rabid Goblin collapses, exhausted.

Rabid Goblin drops **2 glittered pebbles**.

If you want to keep them, note you have gained **2 glittered pebbles**.

If you leave by the north portal, go to 344
If you leave by the east portal, go to 390
If you leave by the south portal, go to 476

319

The body turns with a jump. Suddenly one of the cabinet head's eyes snap open!

"My word! Are you really wandering Lyric's dungeons unarmed?" it asks.

A ginger haired pale face responds. "Yes, you are. And wounded?"

"A run in with Lyric herself, no doubt?" suggests a black bearded old face.

"Yes, yes, quite obvious really," tuts a bushy eyebrowed head.

"You're right, we did run into Lyric!" says Kyla. "Hey, are you Ember?"

"What's not obvious," continues the first head, ignoring Kyla's question, "is who won at cards."

"I'm playing myself, see," grunts a young, tanned face, "but I think I'm cheating."

"My left hand has two cards, an eight of diamonds and two of clubs," explains black beard.

"Which means my left hand has obviously won!" barks a bald white head from the top shelf.

"But I think right hand wins," concludes the first head. "Tell me, what do you think?"

You look over the headless man's shoulder. The two left hand cards are indeed the ones the black bearded face said, whilst the right hand has an ace of hearts and five of spades.

If you say you think that left hand has won, go to 345

If you say you think that right hand has won, go to 33

If you say you cannot answer, go to 425

If you decide to attack the headless man whilst his guard is down, go to 411

320

Thinking quick, you blow hard on the **silver whistle**. Then you blow again, as no noise seems to have come out. Desperate, you blow a third time. The hell hounds appear unaffected by the **silver whistle**. Jaws salivating, they close in.

Go to 503

321

Attached to the plaque are two **golden lances,** lay one over the other forming a cross. Beneath them two **blue shields** have been stuck, forming a sort of coat of arms. Both you and Kyla try to prize the weapons off the plaque, but they seem to be stuck not with glue but sorcery. With no way of yet releasing them from the plaque, you cannot take any of these items at the moment.

If you look at the glass cabinet, go to 41

If you make your way to the north door, go to 10

If you leave by the south door, go to 431

322

If you attack Duke Elf, go to 153

If you attack Mysterious Elf, go to 221

323

You brandish the **purple glow** and wrap Mollusc Head in a distorted aura.

Crack! A successful hit.

Mollusc Head moans.

Mollusc Head holds its breath and vibrates.

Closest Mollusc Head bursts in a slimy shower!

You are coated in thick goo.

With a slurping groan, the remaining heads swap places.

Mollusc Head growls and bubbles slime.

Mollusc Head inhales.

Mollusc Head growls and bubbles slime.

Mollusc Head inhales.

If you attack the closest Mollusc Head, go to 29
If you attack the furthest Mollusc Head, go to 89

324

"Hello, what's this? Dinner!" A young, blonde face licks his lips as headless body snatches the jar of **salted spinach** from you.

Deduct jar of **salted spinach** *from your list of items.*

"Hmm-mmm! Dee-lish! You know, I am surprised you're alive," says a spiky haired head as the body hurriedly unlocks each cabinet.

"Lyric placed a portal over that door. It leads into the belly of a liozard," a chubby chopped face shakes its jowls at you. "Sorry, should've warned you!"

"Yes, I should've!" Another head interjects as the body hand-feeds long strands of **salted spinach** to its drooling lines of faces. "I hope I've learned my lesson. Please, take this."

The wizard's body hands you a rolled up piece of cloth.

"This **flying carpet** will let you sail over the liozard's stomach by giving you a few seconds of flight power," beams a spotty face wearing an eye patch. "Pip pip!"

"Look on that table," instructs black beard. "You'll see a

silver whistle and a **blue shield**. The **silver whistle** plays a pretty tune, albeit one you might not dance to. And if you don't both already have a **blue shield** each, well, I advise you make self-defence your first priority."

"You want to find Ember?" booms a deep baritone voice from the lowest shelf. "Find an elevator gargoyle up to the castle floor. Be careful, Lyric's goblins are everywhere."

"Thank you," smiles Kyla. "All of you!"

"Don't suppose you've run into Bubble yet, have you?" asks black beard. "He lives in the garden hologram north of here. A powerful ally against Lyric, you should go see him, too."

Note the new items you have acquired and choose who is to carry them (if you decide to keep them), remembering each character can only take a maximum of six items each.

"Well, nice to meet you," cheers a stubble bearded face. "Hope you don't get killed. Bye!"

If you leave by the north door, go to 45

If you leave by the east door, go to 431

325

Sai howls and lashes out with beak hands.

Sai misses!

Handsome Elf is unaffected.

If you want Sai to move next:

If you want Sai to attack Handsome Elf, go to 242

If you want Sai to attack Warty Goblin, go to 358

If you want to move next:

If you attack Handsome Elf, go to 494

If you attack Warty Goblin, go to 383

326

You are bathed in foggy light from the **purple glow**.

You are unaffected.

The **purple glow** implodes in thick yellow gas. You can no longer use the **purple glow**.

If you want Zuri to move first:
If you want Zuri to attack Rock Troll, go to 331
If you want Zuri to attack Fire Troll, go to 444
If you want to move first:
If you attack Rock Troll, go to 355
If you attack Fire Troll, go to 369

327

Kyla raises the **purple stick** and casts a 'DEEP BOLT' spell on Rabid Goblin.

Bang! A stunning hit.

Rabid Goblin collapses, exhausted.

Rabid Goblin drops **2 glittered pebbles**.

If you want to keep them, note you have gained **2 glittered pebbles**.

If you leave by the north portal, go to 344
If you leave by the east portal, go to 390
If you leave by the south portal, go to 476

328

The room below is dark, walls smell of damp, the lower ladder rungs dangerously wet. You can just make out a large, iron bar cage running the entire south wall's breadth. Behind it are two steel chests. You see a door in the west wall, but this ladder also carries on down to a lower level. The sewers. Quickening your descent, you miss a rung and, foot flailing, hands slip free. You are falling, hurtling through the blackness, down into the dungeon sewers.

Go to 39

329

Zuri attacks Rock Troll.
Zuri misses!
Rock Troll is unaffected.

Go to 255

330

Before the death blow can be struck, the **purple glow** completely engulfs you. Its light becomes liquid and swells up your mouth, nose and ears. You squeeze shut your eyes but find you are blinded by its sticky shine. In moments, you are completely mummified by the magical weapon.

Such is the strange energy of the **purple glow**. Rather than see its wielder killed, it has you frozen in eternal stasis, unable to move, to the outside world appearing no more than a statue or monument. Soon it will be forgotten you were ever a living being at all. You'll exist forever, only your own thoughts for company, dreaming of the days when Kyla, Adrienne and you were still together.

331

Zuri attacks Rock Troll.
Bang! A stunning hit.
The **rock shield** cracks and snaps in two. Rock Troll can no longer use the **rock shield**.

Rock Troll is bleeding.

Fire Troll raises the **purple stick** and casts a 'DEEP HEAL' spell on Rock Troll.

Rock Troll is fine.

You move next.

If you attack Rock Troll, go to 343

If you attack Fire Troll, go to 353

332

You place your hands on the ladder and put your foot on the first rung. "If I'm wrong, I'll use **cobra bracelet** to return. Goodbye, Sai. Thanks for everything you've done."

"You're a fool," Sai shakes his head. "You're making a big mistake."

Without a reply, you start your way down the ladder, back into Lyric's dungeon pit.

Go to 328

333

You attack Rock Troll.

Crack! A successful hit.

Rock Troll collapses, exhausted.

Rock Troll drops **4 glittered pebbles**.

(You can hold up to **20 glittered pebbles** *and together they will still count as only one item). If you want to keep them, note you have gained* **4 glittered pebbles**.

Cackling Goblin beats his chest and hollers for help.

White Bearded Man comes to his aid!

Cackling Goblin attacks Zuri.

Cackling Goblin misses!

Zuri is unaffected.

Zuri moves next.

If you want Zuri to attack Cackling Goblin, go to 341

If you want Zuri to attack White Bearded Man, go to 363

334

Kyla raises the **purple stick** and casts a **'DEEP BOLT'** spell on Hob Goblin.

Bang! A stunning hit.

Hob Goblin collapses, exhausted.

Hob Goblin drops **2 glittered pebbles**.

If you want to keep them, note you have gained **2 glittered pebbles**.

If you leave by the west door, go to 514

If you leave by the east door, go to 209

If you leave by the south door, go to 450

335

You brandish the **purple glow** and wrap Mollusc Head in a distorted aura.

Crack! A successful hit.

Mollusc Head moans.

Mollusc Head holds its breath and vibrates.

Closest Mollusc Head bursts in a slimy shower!

You are coated in thick goo.

With a slurping groan, the remaining heads swap places.

Mollusc Head growls and bubbles slime.

Mollusc Head inhales.

Mollusc Head growls and bubbles slime.

Mollusc Head inhales.

If you attack the closest Mollusc Head, go to 351

If you attack the furthest Mollusc Head, go to 89

336

"Are you Ember the wizard?" Kyla asks, cautiously. At first there is no answer. You give the **knitted puppet** a prod with the ladle.

"Gerroff! No, I'm not Ember, OK? I'm not a wizard at all. Lyric put a curse on me. Thought rather than kill me, she'd try out an experiment. Bit like her chamber of flesh - seen that yet? Thank hell I didn't end up there. No, I got put into a state of stasis and my soul trapped in this stupid voodoo doll. Seen that body over there? That's me. Not all goblins serve Lyric willingly, right?"

"Lyric attacked us, that's how I got hurt," ventures Kyla. "She took Adrienne. A goat boy told us that the wizard Ember could help us. Do you know where he is?"

"Goat boy? Sounds like Filth. My mate. Since Lyric did this to us, he's been looking after my kitchen, looking after my body, all that. Tidiest guy I ever met. Braver than Ember; that coward hides himself away down in the dungeon sewers. Talk about dirty, right?"

"Can you direct us to the sewers?" you ask the **knitted puppet**.

"Maybe. I dunno. You colour blind? We don't want nothing to do with no colour blinders here."

If you say you are colour blind, go to 77
If you say you are not colour blind, go to 93

337

You brandish the **purple glow** and wrap Hob Goblin in a distorted aura.

Bang! A stunning hit.

The **blue shield** is crushed to dust. Hob Goblin can no longer use the **blue shield**.

Hob Goblin collapses, exhausted.

Hob Goblin drops **2 glittered pebbles**.

If you want to keep them, note you have gained **2 glittered pebbles**.

If you leave by the west door, go to 514
If you leave by the east door, go to 209
If you leave by the south door, go to 450

338

Zuri attacks Fire Troll.

Zuri misses!

Fire Troll is unaffected.

Go to 255

339

✒ Fight!

Queen Elf   (Weapons: **golden lance / golden shield**)
Mysterious Elf   (Weapons: **purple stick / golden shield**)
Duke Elf   (Weapons: **purple stick / golden shield**)

Mysterious Elf raises the **purple stick** and casts a '**DEEP BOLT**' spell on you.

If you have cobra shield, go to 526
If you have a purple glow, go to 421
If you have neither, go to 401

340

You invoke the spirit of Ember and slice at Clawed Dragon with **cobra sceptre**!

A small chunk of scaled armour falls from Clawed Dragon's belly.

Clawed Dragon is bleeding.

Lyric leaps down from Clawed Dragon's back.

Clawed Dragon spews a ball of fire at you.

You are engulfed in a blaze.

The **purple glow** implodes in thick yellow gas. You can no longer use the **purple glow**.

You are bleeding.

Sai moves next.

If you want Sai to attack Lyric, go to 106
If you want Sai to attack Clawed Dragon, go to 267

341

Zuri attacks Cackling Goblin.

Bang! A stunning hit.

Cackling Goblin collapses, exhausted.

Cackling Goblin drops **1 glittered pebble**.

If you want to keep it, note you have gained **1 glittered pebble**.

White Bearded Man wiggles his fingers and casts a '**DEEP MIRAGE**' spell.

White Bearded Man turns to Warm Potato Pie.

You attack Warm Potato Pie.

Crack! A successful hit.

White Bearded Man collapses, exhausted.

White Bearded Man drops a jar of **salted spinach**.

If you want to keep it, note you have gained a jar of **salted spinach**.

Go to 295

342

If you want Adrienne to attack Clawed Dragon, go to 257
If you want Adrienne to heal herself, go to 243
If you want Adrienne to heal Sai, go to 269
If you want Adrienne to heal you, go to 495

343

You attack Rock Troll.

You miss!

Rock Troll is unaffected.

Go to 255

344

Somebody has locked this portal. You hear a faint chuckling within. You can't pass this way right now.

Go to 514

345

"Yes!" beams a cheerful face on the middle shelf. "That's definitely right. I told myself so!"

"Pa pa pa pa," huffs a long, blond haired head beside it.

"Thank you for helping me with that one," says black beard. "Very kind and all that. Ember you're after, eh? No friend of

Lyric, that one. You'll need some defence, you know."

"Look in those trunks by the north door," advises cheerful face. "You'll find yourself a **blue shield** and something to help you past the liozard."

"Right, new game, I think," grins a freckled boy's head. "Toodle pip."

If you make your way toward the north door, go to 426
If you go back through the east door, go to 237

346

With a quiet tick, the case opens. Inside is a **silver ring**. It fits you perfectly. You ask Sai if it's magic.

"No, just a plain old piece of jewellery. Still, it's a nice ring, isn't it? I'd keep it."

You do not have to keep the **silver ring***, although as it fits around your finger you may take it in addition to the other six items you can carry. The* **tin box** *is now empty.*
Go to 246

347

"Ding dong! Off you go," the elevator gargoyle groans. He chucks you out and into the castle tower. This circular, grey brick room has no doors but an incredibly high arched ceiling, stretching way above your head. Wicked-looking instruments of torture dangle from every available space, and caught in the mouths of half-closed iron maidens and open fire places are the severed remains of Lyric's many victims. **Golden lance** raised, the Queen elf herself stands central, two elite guards either side of her spindly frame.

"Welcome, friends!" Lyric purrs. "Not often I receive guests so willingly to my abuse suite."

"Let Adrienne go," you demand. "She's done nothing wrong."

"Adrienne? Ha! She's long dead," cackles the Queen elf. "You ready to follow her to the grave?"

Go to 339

348

"Here it is!" laughs Kyla, climbing to the table and pulling **cobra sceptre** from the glass cabinet.

No one but you can use **cobra sceptre***. Even stronger than* **purple glow** *in battle, this weapon, blessed by Ember, is the final key to taking on the Queen elf. You should still keep the* **purple glow** *for the time being, to use as a shield for when you are attacked.*

At that moment the head collection's owner, a headless wizard in blue robes, enters the room.

"Help me!" cries a dark haired face from the mound of heads piled up about the floor. "I'm drying up!"

"Get a move on," snaps another, as the body frantically starts returning his heads to their cabinet.

"Time to go," advises Kyla. "Next stop, Lyric's abuse suite!"

If you leave by the north door, go to 2
If you leave by the east door, go to 431

349

Sai howls and lashes out with beak hands.

Bang! A stunning hit.

Massive Elf collapses, exhausted.

Massive Elf drops **6 glittered pebbles**.

If you want to keep them, note you have gained **6 glittered pebbles**.

Go to 16

350

If you apply the red paste to her lips, go to 20

If you apply the green paste to her lips, go to 189

If you apply the purple paste to her lips, go to 81

If you change your mind and don't want to risk guessing, go to 97

351

You brandish the **purple glow** and wrap Mollusc Head in a distorted aura.

Crack! A successful hit.

Mollusc Head moans.

Mollusc Head holds its breath and vibrates.

Furthest Mollusc Head bursts in a slimy shower!

You are coated in thick goo.

Mollusc Head roars and vomits projectile acid.

Smash! An outstanding hit.

The **purple glow** implodes in thick yellow gas. You can no longer use the **purple glow**.

You are bleeding.

You attack closest Mollusc Head, go to 14

352

"Woe is me!" The elevator gargoyle descends. "You again? Just my luck. Pah! Going up."

"This is it!" Kyla grabs your hand. "We're really going to save Adrienne!"

If you ask elevator gargoyle to go up to the castle ground floor, go to 386

If you ask elevator gargoyle to go up to the tower, go to 347

353

You attack Fire Troll.

You miss!

Fire Troll is unaffected.

Go to 255

354

"No!" Lyric staggers back, a look of amazement grasping her dying face. "You don't... you fools! You don't even know what you've done..."

The Queen elf is dead. You have won!

"Dead..." Sai drops to his knees. "We did it. We really did it! Where the whole Rebellion failed, we succeeded. Friends, we did it! Lyric is dead!"

"So is Kyla," replies Adrienne. You move to put an arm around her but she pushes you away.

"Yes, Kyla," Sai lowers his tone respectfully. "Adrienne, all I can say is that she died for the noblest of causes. We have prevented Lyric's war. So many will live because of her sacrifice."

"I'll tell that to her parents, shall I?" Adrienne snaps back, turning away from the magitright. "When I'm explaining why she won't be with them this Christmas. How do we explain this to anyone?"

"I don't think we can." You take a deep breath. "Only Kyla knew the **'DEEP PORTAL'** spell to return home. Without her or Ember to guide us, I don't know how we can leave. We're trapped."

Go to 169

355

You attack Rock Troll.

Crack! A successful hit.

The **rock shield** cracks and snaps in two. Rock Troll can no longer use the **rock shield**.

Rock Troll is bleeding.

Fire Troll raises the **purple stick** and casts a '**DEEP HEAL**' spell on Rock Troll.

Rock Troll is fine.

Zuri moves next.

If you want Zuri to attack Rock Troll, go to 329

If you want Zuri to attack Fire Troll, go to 338

356

"I'm hungry!" moans black beard. "It must be time for dinner now."

"Now I'm speaking sense," pipes up scarred face, and several others mutter their agreement.

"It takes lots of salt and lots of calcium for one body to support so many heads," young, tanned face explains. "Sometimes I wish I had two bodies to look after me, but that would be ridiculous."

"If you'll fetch me some extra **salted spinach**, you'll be doing me a great service," the first head says. "There is a Fairy I know who deals in such things. Would you go for me, please?"

If you say you will, go to 392

If you apologise but explain you must find Adrienne, go to 38

357

You are bathed in foggy light from the **purple glow**.

You are unaffected.

If you have cobra sceptre, go to 302

If you want to attack but do not have cobra sceptre, go to 337

If you want Kyla to cast a spell, go to 334

358

Sai howls and lashes out with beak hands.

Crack! A successful hit.

Warty Goblin collapses, exhausted.

Warty Goblin drops **1 glittered pebble**.

(You can hold up to **20 glittered pebbles** *and together they will still count as only one item). If you want to keep it, note you have gained* **1 glittered pebble**.

Go to 509

359

With a soft cough, Freja dies. Sai leaps to his feet, his cockerel and lizard heads snapping in fury.

"Another of us murdered by that evil witch!" he curses. "Friends, I would be lying if I claimed to share your confidence. I have seen the Rebellion wiped out in just one battle. But I would rather die fighting than become one of Lyric's slaves again. To the castle tower! To war!"

You, Sai and Kyla climb aboard the elevator gargoyle.

"Lyric..." Kyla mumbles, chewing her thumb nail. Together you rise, up to Lyric's abuse suite.

Go to 406

360

To your confusion, the elf is happy. You and Sai kneel beside his broken body.

"To die serving our Queen is an honour," he weakly croaks. "Now, my place in the heavens is secured. Unlike you, halflings. To die opposing our spiritually chosen leader guarantees you nothing but an eternity in the flames of the underworld!" With a smile on his face, the elf guard dies.

"Sai? Look, Freja, Sai is bleeding."

You look up to see two women hurrying over from the door in the east wall. One is a skinny female goblin. The other, the owner of the voice you just heard, is a tall, black skinned creature with long, webbed fingers and a gilled neck. Sai seems to recognise them both.

"Friends!" he exclaims. "Freja, Kobbi. Come see our new champion of the Rebellion!"

Go to 464

361

Zuri attacks Cackling Goblin.

Bang! A stunning hit.

Cackling Goblin collapses, exhausted.

Go to 255

362

Duke Elf raises the **purple stick** and casts a **'DEEP INFERNO'** spell on you, Kyla and Sai.

Smash! An outstanding hit.

Sai collapses, exhausted.

Smash! An outstanding hit.

Kyla collapses, exhausted.

Smash! An outstanding hit.

Cobra shield implodes in thick yellow gas. You can no longer use **cobra shield**.

You are bleeding.

Go to 520

363

Zuri attacks White Bearded Man.

Bang! A stunning hit.

White Bearded Man collapses, exhausted.

Go to 309

364

Adrienne attacks Swift Elf.

Swift Elf successfully defends herself with the **golden shield**.

Swift Elf is unaffected.

Go to 166

365

You untie and read the **scroll tied with string.**

"I, the wizard Ember, live through you now at this, the moment before your ultimate victory. To aid your advance, I teach Kyla the **'DEEP INFERNO'** spell. Use it to attack the enemy. You may cast this spell up to four times per battle. Stay strong against Lyric, comrades, you are our final hope. I can advise you no longer... Ember."

Go to 359

366

You attack Cackling Goblin.

Crack! A successful hit.

Cackling Goblin collapses, exhausted.

Go to 255

367

"No one listens to us elders any more!" he complains. "I used to be a knight, now no one... um... what's the word? No one... respects me! I even slew a... um... one of those... things... chopped its big red head right off, you see. I... um... oh, I forget. Who are you? Go away!"

Go to 253

368

The trunk contains several items.

Now Kyla is back the number you can carry returns to six each.

One item is a **scroll tied with string**. Another is a **purple stick**.

You cannot use the **purple stick**, *but Kyla can equip it to cast spells like* **'DEEP PORTAL'**.

Kyla equips herself with the **purple stick**.

You untie and read the **scroll tied with string.**

"I, the wizard Ember, have foreseen your plight, brave ones. Adrienne is alive! Find **cobra sceptre** then head to the tower. To aid your advance, I teach Kyla the **'DEEP BOLT'** spell. Use it to attack the enemy. You may cast this spell up to three times per battle. Stay strong against Lyric, comrades, you are our final hope... Ember."

You also find **3 glittered pebbles** and a **blue shield**.

Note: Kyla is unable to equip **purple glow,** **metal club** *or* **icy stick**. *Only you can use these items.*
You leave by the west door, go to 442

369

You attack Fire Troll.

Crack! A successful hit.

The **rock shield** cracks and snaps in two. Fire Troll can no longer use the **rock shield**.

Fire Troll is bleeding.

Fire Troll raises the **purple stick** and casts a '**DEEP HEAL**' spell on herself.

Fire Troll is fine.

Zuri moves next.

If you want Zuri to attack Rock Troll, go to 329

If you want Zuri to attack Fire Troll, go to 338

370

"Zuri! Help me!"

The monster seizes your throat in its teeth and tears it open. Your hands go weak and fall away as blood gushes down your body. The last words you hear are Zuri's as he attempts to battle on.

"For the Rebellion! For the King!"

Go to 194

371

You brandish the **purple glow** and wrap Handsome Elf in a distorted aura.

Crack! A successful hit.

The **golden shield** is crushed to dust. Handsome Elf can no longer use the **golden shield**.

Handsome Elf is bleeding.

Handsome Elf beats his chest and hollers for help.

Warty Goblin comes to his aid!

Warty Goblin attacks Sai.

Sai giggles and skips out of range.

Sai is unaffected.

Sai moves next.

If you want Sai to attack Handsome Elf, go to 325

If you want Sai to attack Warty Goblin, go to 358

372

Cobra bracelet glows. Inside the steel trunk is a **slab of glittered marble**.

This panel is a **slab of glittered marble** *save point. Make a separate note of the items and spells you and your companion/s are carrying now. At any point from now on, you can return back through time to panel* **372***, minus any items or spells you collect after saving your adventure here. Remember, if you prefer, you can still travel back in time to the save points at panels* **220** *or* **382** *whenever you please.*

You open the second trunk, go to 368

373

Adrienne raises the **purple stick** and casts a '**DEEP HEAL**' spell on herself.

Adrienne is fine.

Go to 496

374

"We have lots of planning to do, so we'd better get back to headquarters. See you soon!"

Kobbi and Freja leave by the door in the east wall of the room.

Go to 473

375

You brandish the **purple glow** and wrap Handsome Elf in a distorted aura.

Crack! A successful hit.

The **golden shield** is crushed to dust. Handsome Elf can no longer use the **golden shield**.

Handsome Elf is bleeding.

If you want Sai to move next:

If you want Sai to attack Handsome Elf, go to 242

If you want Sai to attack Warty Goblin, go to 358

If you want to move next:

If you attack Handsome Elf, go to 494

If you attack Warty Goblin, go to 383

376

✒ Fight!

Queen Elf   (Weapons: **golden lance / golden shield**)

You   (Weapons: none)

Kyla   (Weapons: none)

Adrienne   (Weapons: **metal club**)

Queen Elf attacks Kyla.

Crack! A successful hit.

Kyla is bleeding.

If you want Kyla to counter attack, go to 311

If you want Adrienne to counter attack, go to 191

If you want to counter attack, go to 174

377

"Where is it? It must be in here somewhere!"

"Keep your voice down or someone'll hear us. You're always so loud!"

"Shut up and help. We're close. I can sense it."

Two blue-skinned female elves, both in silver armour, are stood on a table next to a large, glass cabinet. The cabinet contains several rows of severed men's heads. The heads are quite perturbed at their rough treatment by the elves, who are throwing them from the cabinet into a pile in the floor.

"Oh! Oh!" they cry, as they're chucked aside by cruel blue hands. "Ladies, I beg you! Stop!"

"Looking for something, girls?" Kyla shouts to the furtive pair.

The elves freeze, then, in unison, they jolt their heads toward you and Kyla, then back to each other. They leap off the table to face you.

Go to 379

378

You brandish the **purple glow** and wrap Mollusc Head in a distorted aura.

Crack! A successful hit.

Mollusc Head moans.

Mollusc Head holds its breath and vibrates.

Furthest Mollusc Head bursts in a slimy shower!

You are coated in thick goo.

Mollusc Head roars and vomits projectile acid.

You are bathed in foggy light from the **purple glow**.

You are unaffected.

You attack closest Mollusc Head, go to 29

379

✎ Fight!

Fat Elf   (Weapons: **purple glow**)

Whispering Elf   (Weapons: **purple stick / golden shield**)

Whispering Elf raises the **purple stick** and casts a '**DEEP MIRAGE**' spell on herself.

Whispering Elf vanishes!

Fat Elf brandishes the **purple glow** and wraps you in a distorted aura.

If you have cobra shield, go to 121

If you have a purple glow, go to 268

If you have neither of these items, go to 297

380

To your horror, a thick, dark cloud sprays out from the opened trunk and wraps itself around your face. Gagging for air, you try to wave the smoke away, but its intoxicating gas is already filling in your mouth, making it nearly impossible to breathe.

Kyla jumps forward, pulls you back away from the trap and slams the trunk lid down. She asks if you are all right, but your throat is so full of foul magic you are unable to reply.

"Don't worry," Kyla nervously tries to assure you. "I closed it before it got you bad. You're fine."

Your hands pressed to your chest, bent double as you try to regain a normal breath, you are not so certain. Slowly you exhale. What was that thing?

"We shouldn't hang about," Kyla shivers. "Let's go."

If you risk looking in the other trunk, go to 402
If you leave the red rock cavern through the west door, go to 315
If you leave the red rock cavern through the north door, go to 15
If you leave the red rock cavern through the east door, go to 482

381

"What what what?" The magitright pauses and takes a step back. "Another rebel? Comrade!" He goes down on one knee and lowers his head. "With the war looming, so few are brave enough to stand up for what is right. I offer, as recompense for my unprovoked attack, my pledge to champion you against the Queen. Friend, my name is Sai."

Sai the magitright will now fight at your side!
Go to 231

382

Cobra bracelet glows. Inside the steel trunk is a **slab of glittered marble**.

This panel is a **slab of glittered marble** *save point. Make a separate note of the items and spells you and your companion/s are carrying now. At any point from now on, you can return back through time to panel* **382***, minus any items or spells you collect after saving your adventure here. If you prefer, you can still travel back in time to the save point at panel* **220** *whenever you please.*

The steel trunk slides to one side to reveal a hole in the chequered floor. There is a ladder inside it, leading down into a dark pit. You and Sai exchange looks.

"Seems like a trap to me," concludes Sai. "I've been down into the dungeon before, I am definitely not going down there again. No, we're best staying here and preparing a planned attack from rebel base."

If you agree with Sai, go to 473
If you disagree with Sai, go to 90

383

You brandish the **purple glow** and wrap Warty Goblin in a distorted aura.

Crack! A successful hit.

Warty Goblin collapses, exhausted.

Warty Goblin drops **1 glittered pebble**.

(You can hold up to **20 glittered pebbles** *and together they will still count as only one item). If you want to keep it, note you have gained* **1 glittered pebble**.

Go to 509

384

Adrienne complains but has no choice but to follow you and Kyla back down on the elevator gargoyle, out of Lyric's abuse suite and back to the castle floor. Out of the whole Rebellion, only Fairy still lives.

"Hey!" She flutters over as soon as you sees the elevator gargoyle descend. "Where's Sai?"

The three of you explain to Fairy all that has passed. She listens silently as you tell her that her friend is dead. Once you have finished, she lets out a long, slow breath.

"Sai was a great warrior, a brilliant creature. It is my duty to ensure he didn't die for nothing. I will make it my mission to ensure no one takes over this castle as King or Queen." She flutters back over to a large pile of **glittered pebbles** and thoughtfully picks one up. "I will give out all Lyric's gold amongst the people," she decides. "The people don't need a monarch. Together, we will work towards a bright, new age. Yes. That is what Sai would have wanted."

"I really think we should go now." Adrienne grows increasingly anxious and impatient. Kyla nods.

"You're right. Thank you, Fairy, for everything. Good bye, and good luck!"

"Good bye, Fairy." Adrienne takes hold of yours and Kyla's hands and clasps tight. "Let's go."

Kyla raises the **purple stick**.

Finally. She squeezes shut her eyes. "We're going to go home."

Go to 310

385

Kyla raises the **purple stick** and casts a **'DEEP BOLT'** spell on Brigadier Elf.

Bang! A stunning hit.

Brigadier Elf collapses, exhausted.

Brigadier Elf drops **3 glittered pebbles**.

If you want to keep them, note you have gained **3 glittered pebbles**.

If you open the trunk, go to 223

If you look through the window, go to 72

If you leave by the north door, go to 514

If you leave by the east door, go to 450

If you leave by the portal in the south wall, go to 208

386

"Ding dong! Off you go," the elevator gargoyle groans, chucking you off into the castle floor level.

"Sai!"

You see the great magitright sat in the centre of the floor, a skinny female goblin and their tiny Fairy friend beside him. Great tears are rolling down his face. He looks up at you with tired, glazed eyes. "Y... you're alive?" He can hardly believe what he sees. "And... this is..."

"Kyla. I've heard so much about you, Sai. Ember told me. Look - we have **cobra sceptre**!"

Sai shakes his head. "It will be no use. Lyric is too strong. The Rebellion made their attack. We have almost all been wiped out. Kobbi... Zuri... all dead. We tried, but Lyric is too strong. Freja lost her wife in the battle, now her time is near. Lyric will start the war. Everything is lost. All gone."

"No." You grab the magitright's arm firmly. "Get up. We're not beaten yet. Lyric will fall. I swear."

"Yay!" cheers Fairy. "I knew you'd come for us. Ember told me of your destiny. I believe in you!"

If you talk to Freja the goblin, go to 240
If you talk to Fairy, go to 60
If you talk to Sai, go to 270

387

"Pl... please, spare me!" the goat boy gurgles, blood filling his mouth. "I beg you!"

"Leave him alone!" Adrienne steps forward. The goat boy seems surprised, the Queen elf less so. Adrienne crouches beside the goat boy. "Are you all right?"

"Well, well..." A smile on the Queen elf's face looks like a crack on a frozen lake. "And you're good, too. Feisty. Especially this one, all dressed in goblin skin." She gestures toward Adrienne, who is taking off her long, black coat to wrap about the shaking goat boy.

"Who are you?" you ask this strange, blue-skinned woman. Kyla clings to your arm.

The Queen elf's smile caves into a laugh. She raises her **golden lance** again. "I am your new Queen. The war needs strong ones like yourselves. You will come with me now, my new slaves."

Adrienne picks up the goat boy's **metal club**. "I don't know who you are or where we are, but we saw what you did. We're going nowhere."

"Oh, you're spirited. Let's see if your companions share your compassion. Shall we?"
Go to 376

388

You invoke the spirit of Ember and slice Swift Elf in half with **cobra sceptre**!
The **golden shield** is crushed to dust. Swift Elf can no longer use the **golden shield**.
Swift Elf collapses, exhausted.
Swift Elf drops **6 glittered pebbles**.

If you want to keep them, note you have gained **6 glittered pebbles**.

Clawed Dragon beats its chest and hollers for help.

Brute Elf comes to its aid!

Brute Elf attacks you.

Bang! A stunning hit.

Cobra shield implodes in thick yellow gas. You can no longer use **cobra shield**.

You are bleeding.

Kyla raises the **purple stick** and casts a 'DEEP INFERNO' spell on Brute Elf, Clawed Dragon and Lyric.

Smash! An outstanding hit.

Brute Elf collapses, exhausted.

Brute Elf drops **6 glittered pebbles**.

If you want to keep them, note you have gained **6 glittered pebbles**.

Clawed Dragon is out of range.

Clawed Dragon is unaffected.

Lyric is out of range.

Lyric is unaffected.

If you want Kyla to move next, go to 279

If you want Adrienne to move next, go to 197

If you move next, go to 256

389

You brandish the **purple glow** and wrap Brigadier Elf in a distorted aura.

Bang! A stunning hit.

The **golden shield** is crushed to dust. Brigadier Elf can no longer use the **golden shield**.

Brigadier Elf collapses, exhausted.

Brigadier Elf drops **3 glittered pebbles**.

If you want to keep them, note you have gained **3 glittered pebbles**.

If you open the trunk, go to 223

If you look through the window, go to 72

If you leave by the north door, go to 514

If you leave by the east door, go to 450

If you leave by the portal in the south wall, go to 208

390

"Brrrr... it's cold in here," Kyla shivers. "Look at the great, gaping hole in the ceiling."

You stand in front of a circular, purple brick shaft in the room's north wall. Close to where the shaft meets the ceiling there is a large hole in the floor of the room above. There are other exits in this room to the west, south and east. The shaft's entrance is open but nothing is inside. Beside it is a steel trunk.

"Fight!"

From the hole drops a small, red blur. It lands on reptilian feet and uncoils to reveal a brown skinned creature in solid red armour. It licks its lips with a long, forked tongue.

"I am your executioner!" smiles the scaly beast. "The Queen elf's personal Hob goblin, new leader of her goblin army. We have watched your journey with amusement. Ha! You'll proceed no further!"

Go to 213

391

Kyla raises the **purple stick** and casts a **'DEEP INFERNO'** spell on Lyric.

Silence.

Then Lyric emits a piercing scream and dazzling light fills the room.

Lyric collapses, exhausted.

Go to 224

392

"Splendid!" cheers a fat face on the bottom shelf.

"Take a look in those chests by the north door," says black beard as the body points toward the two steel trunks. "My Fairy deals with **glittered pebbles**. You'll find six in the right hand trunk. Use what she asks to buy me the **salted spinach** then spend the change on anything you desire."

"Hey, hold on a minute!" gasps a spotty head with mousy brown hair. "My savings!"

"Oh, be quiet," retorts black beard. "These two are doing me a favour. Oh, you'll find a **blue shield** in there too, best take that in case you run into any of Lyric's undesirables."

"Hey," smiles the first head, warmly, "bring us **salted spinach** in time for dinner, OK?"

If you make your way toward the north door, go to 426
If you go back through the east door, go to 431

393

You brandish the **purple glow** and wrap Mollusc Head in a distorted aura.

Crack! A successful hit.

Mollusc Head moans.

Mollusc Head holds its breath and vibrates.

Closest Mollusc Head bursts in a slimy shower!

You are coated in thick goo.

With a slurping groan, the remaining heads swap places.

Mollusc Head growls and bubbles slime.

Mollusc Head inhales.

Mollusc Head growls and bubbles slime.

Mollusc Head inhales.

If you attack the closest Mollusc Head, go to 443
If you attack the furthest Mollusc Head, go to 89

394

Clawed Dragon swoops!

Clawed Dragon spews a ball of fire at Kyla.

Kyla is engulfed in a blaze.

The **blue shield** cracks and snaps in two. Kyla can no longer use the **blue shield**.

Kyla collapses, exhausted.

Go to 234

395

Smash! An outstanding hit.

The **blue shield** cracks and snaps in two. You can no longer use the **blue shield**.

You are bleeding.

Handsome Elf beats his chest and hollers for help.

Warty Goblin comes to his aid!

Go to 508

396

You brandish the **purple glow** and wrap Mollusc Head in a distorted aura.

Crack! A successful hit.

Mollusc Head moans.

Mollusc Head holds its breath and vibrates.

Closest Mollusc Head bursts in a slimy shower!

You are coated in thick goo.

With a slurping groan, the remaining heads swap places.

Mollusc Head growls and bubbles slime.

Mollusc Head inhales.

Mollusc Head growls and bubbles slime.

Mollusc Head inhales.

If you attack the closest Mollusc Head, go to 516

If you attack the furthest Mollusc Head, go to 89

397

You return to the dim-lit room with the hole down to the sewers. Above is the hole up to the castle level but the ladder is still gone.

The two trunks to the south wall are empty.

Nothing else is here.

You leave by the west door, go to 442

398

You brandish the **purple glow** and wrap Mollusc Head in a

distorted aura.

Crack! A successful hit.

Mollusc Head moans.

Mollusc Head beats his chest and hollers for help.

Nothing happens.

With a slurping groan, neon Mollusc Head exchanges places with the head in front of it.

Mollusc Head growls and bubbles slime.

Mollusc Head inhales.

If you attack the closest Mollusc Head, go to 178

If you attack the middle Mollusc Head, go to 335

If you attack the furthest Mollusc Head, go to 323

399

If you speak to the tall elf, go to 288

If you speak to the walking tree lady, go to 271

If you speak to the stumpy female goblin, go to 481

If you speak to the skinny female goblin, go to 491

If you speak to Fairy, go to 228

If you speak to the female magitright, go to 238

If you speak to the goat boy, go to 479

If you step onto the elevator gargoyle, go to 291

If you make your way to the west door, go to 505

If you make your way to the south door, go to 298

400

You are bathed in foggy light from the **purple glow**.

You are unaffected.

If you want Kyla to cast a spell, go to 385

If you want to attack,

If you have cobra sceptre, go to 307

If not, go to 389

401

Bang! A stunning hit.

You are bleeding.

Go to 142

402

This trunk is full of papers.

"Maybe we'll find a map of the dungeon!" Kyla enthuses.

Many of the papers are damp and rotted. Some are written in an unknown language of runes and shapes. One scroll is entitled *'The Black Goblin Myth Exposed'*. Two large books are labelled *'A Spinach Salter's Guide, parts I - VI'*. A small pamphlet covered in red ink stains is called *'Making Bombs From Bambadeen, Weapons From The Purple Poison'*. There are a number of loose pages with the words 'In you, lusty' scribbled down then scribbled out again.

"No, no map here," sighs Kyla. "Which way are we going to go?"

If you look in the other trunk, go to 512

If you leave the red rock cavern through the west door, go to 315

If you leave the red rock cavern through the north door, go to 15

If you leave the red rock cavern through the east door, go to 482

403

Lyric attacks you.

Bang! A stunning hit.

You collapse, exhausted.

Go to 432

404

✎ **Fight!**

Lyric   (Weapons: **golden lance / golden shield**)

Mysterious Elf   (Weapons: **purple stick / golden shield**)

Duke Elf   (Weapons: **purple stick / golden shield**)

Clawed Dragon   (Weapons: none)

Adrienne   (Weapons: none)

Clawed Dragon swoops!

Lyric jumps onto Clawed Dragon's back.

Clawed Dragon soars up and out of range.

Mysterious Elf raises the **purple stick** and casts a '**DEEP INFERNO**' spell on you, Kyla and Sai.

If you have cobra shield, go to 252

If not, go to 156

405

"I am sorry to hear that," the broken painted lady sighs. "If Lyric has taken this Adrienne, I have to say I think she's unlikely to be alive now. Your best bet is to find Ember. He will be able to send you two back home. Find a way down to the sewers of this dungeon and he will find you. Good luck!"

You thank the broken painted lady for her advice and turn back to the room.

Go to 97

406

"Ding dong! Off you go," the elevator gargoyle groans and throws you into the castle tower.

Its circular grey brickwork has no other exits. A high, arched ceiling stretches way above your head. Wicked-looking instruments of torture dangle from every available space. Caught in the mouths of open fire places and half-closed iron maidens are the severed remains of Lyric's many victims. No sign of the Queen elf. No sign of Adrienne.

"Over here, a steel trunk!" Sai announces.

You open the steel trunk, go to 410

407

The slug pounds down upon you, snapping, drooling acidic vomit. You batter its soft belly with bruised fists, screaming as sick sizzles your flesh, runs in your eyeballs. The mollusc now on top of your chest, you're crushed beneath its massive weight, yet still manage to swing a roundhouse punch that connects with its tender side. The creature bursts, its warm innards gushing out in a hot stream of blood and gore. You feel the liquid washing over you. Everything goes hazy.

You awake sometime later in your new body. You now have three heads. Each is involuntarily regurgitating thick, bubbling slime, ready to attack any other fools who enter this world between worlds. You have been transmorphed into a dream mollusc, vile guardian between the lands of the living and dead, to serve Lyric eternally by ensuring even those who die do not escape her torture. Your only blessing is, after a few years, your memories will fade, until you are unaware you once had any existence other than sentinel to the Queen elf for all time.

408

You cross your fingers and hope for the best.

Go to 277

409

"Kyla... I.... ugh... ..."

"Adrienne! That's her voice!" You spin around. "Where is she?"

"I smell magic here," Kyla mutters. "Lyric is near."

"Nearer than you think!"

An unmistakable cackle fills the air. The **'DEEP MIRAGE'** spell drops and, what you believed to be a bed of nails, an iron chained rack and tomb transmorph into the Queen elf and her two sidekicks. You have been ambushed! A grey shadow across the ceiling fades to reveal a great, winged dragon, smoke pouring from its nostrils. Strapped to a wooden pillar with thick rope you now see Adrienne. Dressed only in torn underwear, her skin's covered in rashes and bruises. Her face is tear-stained.

"Adrienne! My god, what have you done to her? You... you..."

"Go!" croaks Adrienne, her throat dry and weak. "Get out. She..."

"Never!" you roar, brandishing **cobra sceptre**. "This ends here Lyric. You're finished."

"Finished? Ha!" Lyric raises her arms above her head. "You don't know who you are speaking to! I am Lyric. Lyric the indestructible. Lyric the dragon slayer."

"What? dragons... impossible!" Sai looks up at the great beast hovering in the rafters above.

"Yes, dragons!" Lyric gloats, signally for her soldiers to ready their weapons. "To defeat King Dorho I single handedly slaughtered every dragon of Dragon Claw Keep. Every single one. Do you have that power? Do you really think you can beat me, where an army of dragons failed and died? I don't think so. Ha ha ha! Guards, kill them!"
Go to 404

410

Cobra bracelet glows. Inside the steel trunk is a **slab of glittered marble**.

*This panel is a **slab of glittered marble** save point. Make a separate note of the items and spells you and your companion/s are carrying now. At any point from now on, you can return back through time to panel **410**, minus any items or spells you collect after saving your adventure here. Remember, if you prefer, you can still travel back in time to the save points at panels **220**, **372** or **382** whenever you please.*
Go to 409

411

✐ **Fight!**

Headless Figure   (Weapons: **purple stick / blue shield**)

If you have any new weapons / shields you may equip them here.
If you want Kyla to move first, go to 40
If you want to move first, go to 69

412

Sai howls and lashes out with beak hands.

Crack! A successful hit.

Duke Elf collapses, exhausted.

Duke Elf drops **purple stick**.

Duke Elf drops **golden shield**.

Duke Elf drops **10 glittered pebbles**.

Duke Elf's magical hold over Adrienne has been broken!

Adrienne picks up and equips **purple stick**.

Adrienne picks up and equips **golden shield**.

Adrienne picks up **10 glittered pebbles**.

Adrienne will now fight at your side!

You move next. Go to 145

413

Inside are a great number of tins and bottles of powders and pastes, many with damp or peeling labels describing their contents in an unknown text. One box contains nothing but glass tubes full of green eyeballs. Another contains a rolled up piece of parchment, '*Recipe For Mud Sponge Bake*'. A big cardboard carton contains a dozen jars of extra **salted spinach**.

If you want, you can take one jar or more of extra **salted spinach**, *however remember you and Kyla can only carry a maximum of six items each. Each jar counts as one item. If you decide to take any* **salted spinach**, *note how many you take on your item lists.*

Nothing else inside worth investigating, you close the larder door.

If you examine the body of the goblin, go to 85

If you leave by the north door, go to 451

If you leave by the south door, go to 206

414

This must be the same hole Hob goblin leapt through when he made his surprise attack. Leaping down through the gap, you find you do not have Hob goblin's agility, and you land awkwardly on the hard ground below. You lose your balance and cry out in agony. It feels like your ankle is broken!

"Not a good idea!" Sai calls down from the room above. "You'll be goblin food in no time if you can't move quick. Guess we found **cobra bracelet** just in time."

Nodding in deep pain, you squeeze **cobra bracelet** and rewind time!

Go to 220

415

"Sick!" spits the **knitted puppet**. "I knew you were one of them. Don't even touch me, I don't want to catch it off you, colour blinder."

"But..."

"I'm not interested, right? Bog off, no eye!"

Frustrated, Kyla picks up the ladle and bats the **knitted puppet** on the head before turning away from the cauldron.

"Who needs some dead goblin's help anyway? We're doing fine without him!"

Go to 42

416

Kyla successfully defends herself with the **blue shield**.

Kyla is unaffected.

Clawed Dragon beats its chest and hollers for help.

Swift Elf comes to its aid!

Clawed Dragon soars up and out of range.

If you want Sai to move next, go to 188

If you want Kyla to move next, go to 139

If you want Adrienne to move next, go to 124

If you move next, go to 211

417

Sai howls and lashes out with beak hands.

Bang! A stunning hit.

Lyric is bleeding.

Lyric attacks you.

Bang! A stunning hit.

Cobra bracelet is caught by the **golden lance**. **Cobra bracelet** snaps in two.

You can no longer use **cobra bracelet** to travel through time.

You are bleeding.

If you have a gold ring, multiply the stars by the planets and go to that panel

If you do not have a gold ring, go to 125

418

Freja raises the **purple stick** and casts a **'DEEP HEAL'** spell on you.

You are fine.

Freja raises the **purple stick** and casts a **'DEEP HEAL'** spell on Sai.

Sai is fine.

Freja raises the **purple stick** and casts a **'DEEP HEAL'** spell on Kyla.

Kyla is fine.

If you talk to Fairy, go to 60

If you talk to Sai, go to 270

If you return to the elevator gargoyle, go to 519

419

Adrienne raises the **purple stick** and casts a **'DEEP HEAL'** spell on Sai.

Sai is fine.

Go to 496

420

"Yum yum yum!" the black bearded face licks his lips as the wizard's body eagerly takes the jar of **salted spinach** from you.

Deduct this now from your list of items.

"Ah, bliss!" slurps a young, blonde head as the body unlocks one of the cabinets and begins to feed his heads from the jar. "My favourite dish! You really are kind, I don't know how to thank you."

"I do," another head interjects. "You want to find Ember, right? Before you can get to the sewers you'll need to go to castle floor. Find an elevator gargoyle up. You'll find Ember all right."

"Thank you," smiles Kyla, "All of you!"

"Oh, it's nothing," booms a deep baritone voice from the lowest shelf. "Don't suppose you've run into Bubble yet, have you? There's an ally not to be passed by."

"Don't be put off by Bubble's ways," says black beard. "He may growl a little but you won't find anyone more strongly opposed to Lyric than he. He lives in the garden hologram north of here."

The body then hands you a rolled up piece of cloth.

"This **flying carpet** will let you sail over the liozard's stomach by giving you a few seconds of flight power," beams a spotty face wearing an eye patch. "Pip pip!"

Note on your items list that you now have a **flying carpet**.

If you leave by the north door, go to 45
If you leave by the east door, go to 431

421

Smash! An outstanding hit.

The **purple glow** implodes in thick yellow gas. You can no longer use the **purple glow**.

You are bleeding.

Go to 142

422

You invoke the spirit of Ember and slice Swift Elf in half with **cobra sceptre**!

The **golden shield** is crushed to dust. Swift Elf can no longer use the **golden shield**.

Swift Elf collapses, exhausted.

Swift Elf drops **6 glittered pebbles**.

If you want to keep them, note you have gained **6 glittered pebbles**.

Clawed Dragon beats its chest and hollers for help.

Brute Elf comes to its aid!

Brute Elf attacks you.

Bang! A stunning hit.

Cobra shield implodes in thick yellow gas. You can no longer use **cobra shield**.

You are bleeding.

Sai howls and lashes out with beak hands.

Bang! A stunning hit.

Brute Elf collapses, exhausted.

Brute Elf drops **6 glittered pebbles**.

If you want to keep them, note you have gained **6 glittered pebbles**.

If you want Sai to move next, go to 170

If you want Adrienne to move next, go to 342

If you move next, go to 256

423

The trunk contains a **blue shield**.

Either you or Kyla can take this item. Whoever takes it will have extra defence if attacked. Remember, each of you can only carry a maximum of six items at a time.

If you leave by the north door, go to 489

If you go back and leave through the east door, go to 431

424

You hurry out of the chamber of skin into a very different room.

"Slow down!" wheezes Kyla and she struggles in behind you, her hand still pressed tight on the wound she suffered from the battle with Lyric. "Phew! Oh, this is more like it."

You are in a bright but cluttered kitchen. On your left is series of tables, upon which are a variety of quite fresh looking vegetables and several sharp looking knives. To your right is a large bubbling cauldron. Above the cauldron, a long upward tunnel leads through the ceiling and daylight pours through. There are several cupboards and shelves, all full of bowls, plates and jugs, on every wall. Before you are two large doors. The left door is slightly open and is clearly a small larder, full of large boxes and packages. The right door is shut.

"Oh no! Look at that!"

Slumped in the corner, beside the cupboard, is what looks like a dead body. Scaled and dusty, you guess it's the corpse of some sort of goblin. Gingerly you step closer to take a better look.

"God, it stinks. Oh, that is revolting."

"Yeah? Well you ain't so smelling of roses yourself, missy."

You both freeze. The voice did not come from the body. Who was it?

Go to 167

425

"Blasted nonsense, what use is that?" spits an angry face with a scar on its forehead.

"If ace is high, I guess right hand wins," you suggest. "If ace is low, I'd say it was left."

There is a general murmur amongst the heads. The body crosses its arms, in careful thought.

"Smarty pants!" a stubbly chinned face eventually jeers. "No one likes a show-off!"

Go to 356

426

There is a steel trunk either side of the door.

If you open the trunk on the left, go to 13

If you open the trunk on the right, go to 31

If you leave by the north door, go to 489

If you go back and leave through the east door, go to 431

427

Kyla raises the **purple stick** and casts a '**DEEP INFERNO**' spell on Lyric.

Smash! An outstanding hit.

Lyric is bleeding.

Lyric attacks you.

Bang! A stunning hit.

Cobra bracelet is caught by the **golden lance**. **Cobra bracelet** snaps in two.

You can no longer use **cobra bracelet** to travel through time.

You are bleeding.

If you have a gold ring, multiply the stars by the planets and go to that panel

If you do not have a gold ring, go to 148

428

"Reckon your clever? Reckon again! In the chamber of flesh, what colour are the eyes?"

If you say green, go to 306

If you say blue go to 67

429

You brandish the **purple glow** and wrap Whispering Elf in a distorted aura.

Bang! A stunning hit.

The **golden shield** is crushed to dust. Whispering Elf can no longer use the **golden shield**.

Whispering Elf collapses, exhausted.

Whispering Elf drops **6 glittered pebbles**.

If you want to keep them, note you have gained **6 glittered pebbles**.

Go to 348

430

If you want Sai to move next, go to 187
If you want Adrienne to move next, go to 265
If you move next, go to 303

431

"Back where we started," sighs Kyla. The three wooden doors are set into the rock face around you.

If you look in the steel trunks, go to 207
If you leave the red rock cavern through the west door, go to 114
If you leave the red rock cavern through the north door, go to 150
If you leave the red rock cavern through the east door, go to 206

432

"I have discovered how it was you came to be here," Lyric talks down to you, her **golden lance**'s tip resting upon your bleeding neck. Unable to move, you fear you have become paralysed by her assault. "I must say, I am very impressed. You have friends in high places. Sadly, not high enough."

"Please... no..." You screw your eyes up tightly and bite on your lip.

Lyric pulls back her **golden lance** and burrows it deep into your skull. You have been beaten by the Queen elf, lost not only your own chance of getting home but also any hope of freeing this land from her tyranny. War will come. Many will suffer as a result of your failure. The final words you hear are the ecstatic cheers of Lyric's evil army echoing in your head.

"Long live the Queen! Long live the Queen! Long live the Queen!"

433

On the table is a small, blood-stained note book. It is a goblin's diary. It reads: *'Morning, kill. Lunch, then kill. Brush teeth. Kill, then bed.'* There is nothing else of interest in this room.

If you leave by the north door, go to 217
If you leave by the west door, go to 390
If you leave by the south door, go to 475

434

You attack Hob Goblin.

Hob Goblin successfully defends himself with the **blue shield**.
Hob Goblin is unaffected.

Hob Goblin raises the **purple stick** and casts a 'DEEP BOLT'
spell on you.

Bang! A stunning hit.

You collapse, exhausted.

Go to 181

435

A load of dirty clothes are being boiled. Also in the cauldron is a
long, metal ladle.

If you use the ladle to spoon out an item of clothing, go to 493
If you turn your attention back to the rest of the room, go to 190

436

You attack Hob Goblin.

Crack! A successful hit.

The **purple stick** cracks and snaps in two. Hob Goblin can no
longer use the **purple stick**.

Hob Goblin collapses, exhausted.

Hob Goblin drops **1 glittered pebble**.

(You can hold up to **20 glittered pebbles** *and together they will
still count as only one item). If you want to keep it, note you have
gained* **1 glittered pebble**.

Go to 251

437

"My father gave me this **wood box** on his death bed," she tells
you. "Told me that a special weapon was hidden inside ready for

the coming storm. I don't know what he meant. I never did. There is something written on the lid but it don't seem to be the right code for this lock."

You take a look at the **wood box**. On the lid is inscribed *'Left a bit, right a bit, left a bit more.'* There is a dial on the **wood box**. You try this but it does not open. You can't open the **wood box** yet.

"I'm hungry. I might go get some **salted spinach** off Fairy. I know you hate it, Sai, but I can't get enough of the stuff. See you both soon."

You both bid farewell to the elf girl and step back outside.

If you look about the south-most hut, go to 73
If you look about the north-most hut, go to 116
If you return through the gates into the castle, go to 299

438

"Very tough!" Long blue fingers seize Adrienne's arm and pin her close to an armoured chest. "I have a place for this one. Filth, you did well after all."

There is a burst of green smoke around Adrienne and the Queen elf which encases them both. Adrienne tries to speak, but her voice is lost in the spell's dark aura. With a bubbling groan, the smoke sucks in on itself, and with a small imploding 'pop', both women vanish.

"Adrienne!" cries Kyla, clasping her own wound where the Queen elf gashed her side. She turns to the goat boy. "What's happening? Where is she? Where are we?"

"It's my fault," he wheezes, trying but failing to get to his feet. "My name is Filth. Like all in this dungeon, I am Lyric's slave. Lyric, the Queen elf, murdered my old master, the King of Dragon Claw Keep, and took his castle by force. Now, all must serve her in preparation for the war, or die."

"You must rest," you advise Filth. "Don't speak. We'll fetch someone to see to your wounds."

"No, it's too late for me." Filth reaches out for your hand.

"I'm so sorry."

"How did we get here? What's going on?" asks Kyla.

"This is the pit of Lyric's dungeon. I came here to create a magical pentagram, in the hope of escaping her slavery. Your Adrienne - her magic collided with mine and accidentally took you here."

"Adrienne's magic? But-"

"Listen - you're in grave danger. Forget about Adrienne - now Lyric has her captive there is no hope for her now. Go to Ember. He is a strong magician. I heard he is hiding from Lyric in the sewers beneath this dungeon. Ember will help. Just stay away from Lyric's tower. Go... now.... I wish you... good... ...." His final breath spent, Filth dies.

You and Kyla are now alone in Lyric's dungeon.

Go to 3

439

⚔ Fight!

Hell Hound   (Weapons: none)

Hell Hound attacks Sai.
Crack! A successful hit.
Sai is bleeding.
If you want Sai to move first, go to 492
If you want to move first:
If you have a silver whistle and want to use it, go to 275
If you have a bone and want to use it, go to 457
If you have a lucky charm and want to use it, go to 408
Otherwise, go to 286

440

You attack Dribbling Goblin.
Crack! A successful hit.
The **blue shield** cracks and snaps in two. Dribbling Goblin can

no longer use the **blue shield**.

Dribbling Goblin is bleeding.

Muttering Goblin raises the **purple stick** and casts a '**DEEP HEAL**' spell on Dribbling Goblin.

Dribbling Goblin is fine.

Go to 502

441

⚔ Fight!

Magitright   (Weapons: none)

Magitright howls and lashes out with beak hands.

Crack! A successful hit.

The **blue shield** cracks and snaps in two. You can no longer use the **blue shield**.

You are bleeding.

You attack Magitright.

Magitright giggles and skips out of range.

Magitright is unaffected.

Go to 215

442

You and Kyla enter another pitch black chamber. A tiny light flickers above a door to the south. You can see nothing else, but hear a low, guttering growl from somewhere deep in the darkness!

"Do you hear that?" Kyla whispers. "Quickly, let's go!"

If you leave by the south door, go to 138

If you leave by the east door, go to 397

443

You brandish the **purple glow** and wrap Mollusc Head in a distorted aura.

Crack! A successful hit.

Mollusc Head moans.

Mollusc Head holds its breath and vibrates.

Furthest Mollusc Head bursts in a slimy shower!

You are coated in thick goo.

Mollusc Head roars and vomits projectile acid.

Smash! An outstanding hit.

The **purple glow** implodes in thick yellow gas. You can no longer use the **purple glow**.

You are bleeding.

You attack closest Mollusc Head, go to 14

444

Zuri attacks Fire Troll.

Bang! A stunning hit.

The **rock shield** cracks and snaps in two. Fire Troll can no longer use the **rock shield**.

Fire Troll is bleeding.

You move next.

If you attack Rock Troll, go to 343

If you attack Fire Troll, go to 109

445

Adrienne raises the **purple stick** and casts a 'DEEP HEAL' spell on Sai.

Sai is fine.

Go to 55

446

"You see what happens?" the elf laughs manically. "You see what happens when you cross the elite guard! Your Rebellion will be crushed! Say your prayers, mortal."

The broken **purple glow** throbs in your fist. As the elf closes in, it begins to expand around you.

Go to 330

447

You and Kyla enter the headless wizard's marble walled home.

Along the west and south walls are the giant, floor to ceiling glass cabinets with their rows of severed heads. All now have their eyes shut, possibly sleeping. The headless wizard's body is nowhere to be seen.

If you leave by the north door, go to 2
If you leave by the east door, go to 431

448

"You see what happens?" the elf laughs manically. "You see what happens when you cross the elite guard! Your Rebellion will be crushed! Say your prayers, mortal."

Go to 194

449

"Reckon you're clever? Reckon again! In the chamber of flesh, what colour are the eyes?"

If you say green, go to 67
If you say blue go to 198

450

You enter a small, square room with pale blue brick walls. In each wall is a single door. Above, the ceiling is lined with hundreds of long, sharp spears, like a massive jury of guilty fingers pointing down at you. You take another step into the room. A quiet, mechanical whirring sound catches your ear.

"What-?"

You follow Kyla's line of sight. The entire spiked ceiling has started to lower and its deadly spears are gradually closing down upon you.

If you leave by the north door, go to 390

If you leave by the west door, go to 47

If you leave by the east door, go to 475

If you leave by the south door, go to 150

If you hold up your arms to push against the spiked ceiling, go to 485

451

Thud!

"Ow! What happened?"

Lying in a dazed heap on the floor, you look up to see the door through which you just came high up on the wall behind you, a large drop between you and the ground. Kyla landed on her wounded arm.

"**Knitted puppet** could have warned us about that. Hey - look at this place!"

Above you, fixed to the ceiling, is a table and three chairs. In fact, the entire room is upside down! There are three doors leading in, but you cannot reach any of them, as they're all too high above. The ceiling you are standing on is bare, and the pale blue walls are too smooth to climb up.

"Look over there!"

To your right, there is a small platform about halfway up the east wall. A ladder leads up to it. With no other options, you both walk over and climb up onto the ledge. On it are two levers. One is red and one green. A sign above them reads *'Red kills! Do not touch!'*

"What do you think? One of **knitted puppet's** traps to weed out the colour blind, maybe?"

If you pull the green lever, go to 157
If you pull the red lever, go to 201

452

"Bah!" grumbles the **knitted puppet**. "Here's where your lucky streak ends, my colour blind nemesis! Tell me the colour of this purple sock?"

If you say purple, go to 74
If you say something else, go to 24

453

Kyla tries to run to your aid, but the headless wizard easily bats her aside. You sink to the floor as he stands triumphantly above you, weapon raised. When casting his next **'DEEP BOLT'** spell he'll be careful only to incinerate you below the neck. The cabinet will have an extra head tonight.

Go to 194

454

"She's great," you offer. "You're a brilliant artist."

"Liar!" he spits back. "You sycophantic creep! I have a good mind to have you arrested for harassment, tormenting a poor elderly artist in such an embarrassing manner. Get out of my sight!"

Go to 56

455

"Aha!" shouts a spiky haired head from the middle of the shelves.

"Splendid to see you!" remarks another higher up.

"To be honest, I'm surprised you're alive," continues spiky hair. "The portal in that door leads straight into the belly of a liozard. I don't know how to reverse that portal, but I can give you this."

The wizard's body hands you a rolled up piece of cloth.

"This **flying carpet** will let you sail over the liozard's stomach by giving you a few seconds of flight power," beams a face wearing an eye patch. "Pip pip!"

"You should both have one of these too," advices spiky hair, as the wizard's body places a **blue shield** in your hands. "Keep yourself protected and all."

"You wanted Ember..." mutters a quiet, old head. "That's right, eh? Keep north. Ask Bubble."

Remember you can only carry a maximum of six items each, so decide who will get what.

If you leave by the north door, go to 45
If you leave by the east door, go to 431

456

Nothing happens.
If you turn the dial left, go to 5
If you turn the dial right, go to 499
If you do not turn the dial again, go to 246

457

Your body acts almost before your mind has engaged with what it is doing. Instinctively, you raise the **bone** above your head, then hurl it as far as you can. The **bone** ricochets off one of the racks and bounces through the door in the south wall. The hell hound's left head watches the **bone** fly through the air, transfixed, whilst the right head never lets its stare drop from you and Sai. Suddenly, the left head makes a jerk towards the south door. Gagging like someone has their hands round its neck, the right head has no choice but to follow as the beast bounds like a puppy after the thrown **bone.**

"Well done!" chuckles Sai. "I thought we were gonnas! Any more tricks like that up your sleeve?"

Mark the discarded **bone** *off your item list.*
"There's no stopping us now. Let's go!"
If you leave by the north door, go to 65
If you leave by the west door, go to 299
If you leave by the south door, go to 244

458

⚔ Fight!

Mollusc Head   (Weapons: none)
Mollusc Head   (Weapons: none)
Mollusc Head   (Weapons: none)

Mollusc Head growls and bubbles slime.
Mollusc Head inhales.
Mollusc Head growls and bubbles slime.
Mollusc Head inhales.

If you attack the closest Mollusc Head, go to 477
If you attack the middle Mollusc Head, go to 398
If you attack the furthest Mollusc Head, go to 264

459

You brandish the **purple glow** and wrap Mollusc Head in a distorted aura.

Crack! A successful hit.

Mollusc Head moans.

Mollusc Head holds its breath and vibrates.

Closest Mollusc Head bursts in a slimy shower!

You are coated in thick goo.

With a slurping groan, the remaining heads swap places.

Mollusc Head growls and bubbles slime.

Mollusc Head inhales.

Mollusc Head growls and bubbles slime.

Mollusc Head inhales.

If you attack the closest Mollusc Head, go to 443
If you attack the furthest Mollusc Head, go to 89

460

Kyla attacks Bubble.

Pop! A successful hit.

Bubble bursts, exhausted.

Bubble drops **2 glittered pebbles**.

(You can hold up to **20 glittered pebbles** *and together they will still count as only one item). If you want to keep them, note you have gained* **2 glittered pebbles**.

Go to 137

461

As fast as you can, you grab the jar and scoop out a big handful of the sticky paste inside. With far less precision than last time, you throw the paste onto the painted lips. *Splat!* The gooey mess dribbles down the picture and drips off the edge of the golden frame.

Go to 301

462

Inside is a **metal club**.

You can take the **metal club** *if you wish, but remember that now you cannot take more than six items.*

You then step onto the elevator.

Go to 54

463

The hut's door is pulled back, where a young elf girl is sat holding a **wood box**. She waves to Sai.

"Hey, Sai! Come on in, man. I'm trying to figure the combination to this lock. Still no luck!"

If you go in and take a look at the wood box, go to 437

If you look about the south-most hut, go to 73

If you look about the north-most hut, go to 116

If you return through the gates into the castle, go to 299

464

"I am Kobbi, a water troll," the gilled necked woman tells you. "Yes, I am a member of the Rebellion. Please, can Freja attend to the injuries you and Sai have suffered against the elite guard?"

If you say yes, go to 8

If you say no, go to 374

465

Sai howls and lashes out with beak hands.

Silence.

Then Lyric emits a piercing scream and dazzling light fills the room.

Lyric collapses, exhausted.

Go to 354

466

If you have cobra sceptre and wish to offer it to headless wizard, go to 121

If you have a jar of salted spinach and wish to offer it to headless wizard, go to 420

If you have a jar of salted spinach and 5 glittered pebbles to offer headless wizard, go to 324

If you have none of these items to offer or don't want to offer them, go to 455

467

"Vermin, everywhere!" the drooling goblin pants, believing he is talking to his fellow warriors. "I am going to report to Hob goblin. Meet me in the chamber of flesh." He scurries through the door in the west wall just in time, as the '**DEEP MIRAGE**' spell begins to flicker and fade.

Note that now that you have used that spell, it cannot be used again.

If you look at the table by the bed, go to 62

If you leave by the north door, go to 99

If you leave by the west door, go to 390

If you leave by the south door, go to 475

468

There is a scroll inside the trunk.

You unroll it and read: *'The Dream Mollusc cannot harm you when you are awake. Do not sleep! Stay awake tonight.'*

If you leave by the south door, go to 300

If you take the elevator gargoyle back up a level, go to 399

469

You attack Magitright.

Magitright giggles and skips out of range.

Magitright is unaffected.

Magitright howls and lashes out with beak hands.

Crack! A successful hit.

You collapse, exhausted.

Go to 194

470

If you leave by the north door, go to 209

If you leave by the west door, go to 450

If you leave by the south door, through which you came, go to 190

471

✎ Fight!

Drooling Goblin   (Weapons: **icy stick / blue shield**)

Yawning Goblin   (Weapons: **icy stick**)

Itchy Goblin   (Weapons: nothing)

Itchy Goblin attacks Kyla.

Itchy Goblin misses!

Kyla is unaffected.

Yawning Goblin attacks Kyla.

Yawning Goblin misses!

Kyla is unaffected.

If you have any new weapons / shields you may equip them here.

Itchy Goblin and Yawning Goblin are out of range.

If you want Kyla to move first, go to 64

If you want to move first, go to 80

472

"Can't... speak... pain... toooo... uh..."

The sketched lips are exhausted. Neither Kyla nor you know what to say, then a loud snapping noise makes you both jump. You look back to the frame to see the mouth picture has split into pieces. Tiny shreds of canvas fall like confetti to the floor. Behind the now empty frame is a small hatch. It is slightly ajar.

If you open the hatch, go to 52
If you decide not to, go to 97

473

In the gold brick wall opposite, the east door is the only other door out of here. At the moment it is blocked by a large portcullis. The fallen elf's body lies beside the large steel trunk.

If you open the trunk, go to 382
If you leave by the east door, go to 65

474

"Yes, of course. I'm sorry," Zuri apologises. "I was fighting one of Lyric's elite guard, that's how I bust my arm up. Soon as Alchemist has cured me I'm getting back to the Rebellion. I will see you there."

You and Sai bid Zuri farewell and leave his home.

If you look about the west-most hut, go to 463
If you look about the north-most hut, go to 116
If you return through the gates into the castle, go to 299

475

Thud!

Lying in a dazed heap on the floor, you look up to see the door through which you just came high up on the wall behind you. The entire room is upside down. There are three doors leading in, but you cannot reach any of them, as they're all too high above. To your right is a ladder to a small platform about halfway up the east wall. You climb the ladder up and find two levers. One is red and one green. A sign above them reads: *'Red kills! Do not touch!'*

If you pull the green lever, go to 219
If you pull the red lever, go to 201

476

You're in a shiny corridor made of steel. There are two exit doors and a small portal to the south. There's a steel trunk to your left.

The wall to your left has a large barred window in it.

A short elf in a padded coat decorated with many medals stands before you. "For the elite!" he cries.

Go to 9

477

You brandish the **purple glow** and wrap Mollusc Head in a distorted aura.

Crack! A successful hit.

Mollusc Head moans.

Mollusc Head beats his chest and hollers for help.

Nothing happens.

With a slurping groan, neon Mollusc Head exchanges places with the head in front of it.

Mollusc Head growls and bubbles slime.

Mollusc Head inhales.

If you attack the closest Mollusc Head, go to 393

If you attack the middle Mollusc Head, go to 335

If you attack the furthest Mollusc Head, go to 168

478

The body is covered in a thick layer of dust. Its skin is dark green. There is definitely no sign of life.

Go to 167

479

"Have you eaten any of Fairy's **salted spinach**?" asks the goat boy. "Yuck! Here in the Rebellion, we get worse rations than Lyric's slaves. That **salted spinach** turns my stomach."

Go to 399

480

Adrienne raises the **purple stick** and casts a 'DEEP HEAL' spell on you.

You are fine.
Clawed Dragon swoops!
Clawed Dragon spews a ball of fire at Kyla.
Kyla successfully defends herself with the **blue shield**.
Kyla is unaffected.
If you want Kyla to move next, go to 102
If you move next, go to 263

481

"You think all goblins are evil?" she hisses. "I have been against Lyric ever since we heard about the Rebellion. At first my wife would not join me. I was in the first assault against Lyric, where so many of us were killed. I used a **purple glow** in battle, a magic weapon which assumes the shape you require, sword or shield. But unlike a normal shield, it will protect you from magical attack. I lost mine in battle and returned badly hurt. That's when my wife became a healer."
Go to 399

482

The east door takes you to a chamber of similar size to the cavern you just left. There is one other exit, a low archway to the north.

Kyla clasps her hands to her mouth, as if she's about to be sick.

The walls, floor and ceiling around are made from stretched flesh, sewn together at random points by giant black stitches. Twitching and flexing about this skin are hundreds of fingers. Some are close together, almost forming hands. Others are separate, vibrating in spasm or limp and lifeless.

A flapping, hairy hand protruding from the floor takes a swipe at your ankle.

At some points between fingers are single staring eyes, large, lidless, deep blue. Two of these eyes, high on the east wall, are near a thin, open mouth, drooling tongue hanging from toothless gums.

"Come to me!" the mouth hisses, and five outstretched fingers quiver in your direction.

If you take hold of the hand, go to 12

If you leave by the north archway, go to 424

If you leave by the west door, through which you came, go to 237

483

Adrienne raises the **purple stick** and casts a 'DEEP HEAL' spell on Kyla.

Kyla is fine.

Go to 403

484

"This statue is of our old King," he tells you. "It just appeared one day. He had a magic **purple glow** he always took to battle. That's a strong weapon which also protects its user from magical attacks. No need for a sword, staff or shield, a **purple glow** can take on whatever form its wielder requires. Don't know if our great Queen would use such a weapon. She probably has something even better."

Go to 253

485

Strong and defiant, you brace yourself for impact.

"What are you doing?" yells Kyla. "Come on, let's go!" She disappears through the door in the north wall.

Suddenly, pain grips you as the first spears pierce your hands. You look up, see blood trickling down your arms and find yourself pinned to the spot. You are forced down to your knees as the roof continues to descend.

"Kyla!" you call out, but it is too late. Turning your face away from the sharp tips about to dig into your head, you realise there is no escape.

If you have a purple glow, go to 330
Otherwise, go to 194

486

The trunk is empty.
Go to 123

487

Behind the barred window sits a young goat girl.

"Hey there!" she greets. "If you have any **gold coins**, I'll gladly make an exchange!"

golden lance   **4 gold coins**
golden shield   **4 gold coins**

*You don't have any **gold coins**. You can't buy anything yet!*

"Nice to do business with you," she smiles. "See you again."

If you have a wooden bucket and wish to use it, go to 304
If you leave by the north door, go to 137
If you leave by the east door, go to 450
If you leave by the portal in the south wall, go to 208

488

The body is covered in a thick layer of dust. Its skin is dark green. There is definitely no sign of life.
Go to 42

489

No sooner are you both through the door than you find yourselves skidding down a soft, slimy slope. You arrive with a splash in a small, shallow pool of sticky liquid. The pink walls around you look like marshmallow, but marshmallow covered with hundreds of squiggly blue lines.

"Veins!" gasps Kyla. "We're inside some sort of creature's gut! But how?"

A deep gurgling rumbles above your heads and the pink walls quiver.

If you have a flying carpet and want to try using it, go to 121
If you have a lucky charm and want to try using it, go to 522
If you have a bar of soap and want to try using it, go to 70
If you have none of these items, go to 293

490

The **purple glow** implodes in thick yellow gas. You can no longer use the **purple glow**.

You are bleeding.

If you have a silver whistle and want to use it, go to 320
If you have a bone and want to use it, go to 515
If you have a packet of icing sugar and want to use it, go to 408
Otherwise, go to 286

491

"That's right, I trained as a healer to cure my lover's wounds. Give me a moment to prepare myself. I will repair your battle scars before you leave headquarters."

Go to 399

492

Sai howls and lashes out with beak hands.

Crack! A successful hit.

Hell Hound is bleeding.

Go to 503

493

You pull out a **wet sock**.

If you want to keep the **wet sock***, add it to your list of items. Remember, Kyla and you can only carry up to six items each.*

Go to 190

494

You brandish the **purple glow** and wrap Handsome Elf in a distorted aura.

Crack! A successful hit.

Handsome Elf collapses, exhausted.

Handsome Elf drops **5 glittered pebbles**.

(You can hold up to **20 glittered pebbles** *and together they will still count as only one item). If you want to keep them, note you have gained* **5 glittered pebbles***.*

Sai attacks Warty Goblin, go to 511

495

Adrienne raises the **purple stick** and casts a 'DEEP HEAL' spell on you.

You are fine.

Clawed Dragon swoops!

Clawed Dragon spews a ball of fire at Sai.

Sai giggles and skips out of range.

Sai is unaffected.

If you want Sai to move next, go to 183

If you move next, go to 340

496

Lyric attacks you.

Bang! A stunning hit.

You collapse, exhausted.

Go to 432

497

Clunk!

You both land heavily on cold, metal floor. Quickly getting to your feet, you see you're in a shiny corridor made entirely of steel. What look like thin electric lights line the ceiling. There is one solid metal door in the east wall near by you, and a second metal door at the end of the corridor in the north wall. There's a steel trunk to your left. The wall to your left has a large barred window in it.

If you open the trunk, go to 136
If you look through the window, go to 129
If you leave by the north door, go to 193
If you leave by the east door, go to 450
If you leave by the portal in the south wall, go to 179

498

Lyric rushes forward.

If you want Kyla to move next, go to 245
If you want Adrienne to move next, go to 254
If you move next, go to 303

499

The **tin box** will not open. There is a small dial on it.

If you turn the dial left, go to 218
If you turn the dial right, go to 456
If you do not turn the dial, go to 246

500

Thanking her for the spell, you proceed through the door both refreshed and rejuvenated.

If you have met the water troll Kobbi on your travels, go to 473
If you have not yet encountered Kobbi, go to 68

501

"Reckon you're clever? Reckon again! In the chamber of flesh, what colour are the eyes?"

If you say green, go to 67

If you say blue go to 198

502

Dribbling Goblin attacks you.

Crack! A successful hit.

You collapse, exhausted.

Go to 181

503

Hell Hound attacks you.

Crack! A successful hit.

You collapse, exhausted.

Go to 277

504

Skinny Goblin raises the **purple stick** and casts a '**DEEP HEAL**' spell on you.

You are fine.

Skinny Goblin raises the **purple stick** and casts a '**DEEP HEAL**' spell on Sai.

Sai is fine.

Go to 500

505

"Hold on!" the skinny goblin calls as you are about to quit the headquarters. "If you're going back out there you're gonna need a quick boost. Stand still, you two, this won't hurt a bit!"

Go to 504

506
If you have met Alchemist before, go to 507
Otherwise, go to 284

507
The hut is uninhabited. Presumably Alchemist is off completing his rounds.
If you leave by the hut's west door, go to 253
If you leave by the hut's east door, go to 177

508
Warty Goblin attacks you.
Crack! A successful hit.
You collapse, exhausted.
Go to 181

509
Handsome Elf raises the **purple stick** and casts a '**DEEP INFERNO**' spell on you and Sai.
Smash! An outstanding hit.
The **purple glow** implodes in thick yellow gas. You can no longer use the **purple glow**.
You collapse, exhausted.
Smash! An outstanding hit.
Sai collapses, exhausted.
Go to 446

510
"You see what happens?" the elf laughs manically. "You see what happens when you cross the elite guard! Your Rebellion will be crushed! Say your prayers, mortal."

You try to call out for help but the warty goblin sticks a boot into your mouth, smashing in your front teeth. His foot pins you to the ground as your killer raises his **purple stick** and unleashes

a '**DEEP INFERNO**' upon you.
Go to 194

511

Sai howls and lashes out with beak hands.

Crack! A successful hit.

Warty Goblin collapses, exhausted.

Warty Goblin drops **1 glittered pebble**.

If you want to keep it, note you have gained **1 glittered pebble**.

Go to 360

512

This trunk is empty. There is nothing else here to investigate, so you turn your attention to the exits.

If you leave the red rock cavern through the west door, go to 315
If you leave the red rock cavern through the north door, go to 15
If you leave the red rock cavern through the east door, go to 482

513

Crack! A successful hit.

You collapse, exhausted.

Go to 277

514

You are in the holographic garden with its three exit portals.
If you make your way to the north portal, go to 344
If you leave by the east portal, go to 390
If you leave by the south portal, go to 476

515

Your body acts almost before your mind has engaged with what it is doing. Instinctively, you raise the **bone** above your head, then hurl it as far as you can. The hell hounds are not impressed by your **bone**. For a brief moment they stand perfectly still,

staring at you, as if amused by your poor attempt at distraction. Then they resume their attack.
Go to 503

516

You brandish the **purple glow** and wrap Mollusc Head in a distorted aura.

Crack! A successful hit.

Mollusc Head moans.

Mollusc Head holds its breath and vibrates.

Furthest Mollusc Head bursts in a slimy shower!

You are coated in thick goo.

Mollusc Head roars and vomits projectile acid.

Smash! An outstanding hit.

The **purple glow** implodes in thick yellow gas. You can no longer use the **purple glow**.

You are bleeding.

You attack closest Mollusc Head, go to 14

517

The two elves survey yours and Kyla's fallen bodies. The intensity of their attack was so great you are only barely conscious, though conscious enough to see the fat elf's chubby face peering down at you.

"Y'know, I heard some elves from the northern plains reckon there is no greater delicacy than human flesh," she tells her mate. "Big black market over there, see. Knock 'em out, drop 'em in boiling water. Heard it's delicious." She starts licking her lips as she places a cold hand against your cheek. "No one's around. We could do anything! You feel like trying something new?"

Go to 194

518

If you've got a scroll tied with string, go to 365 if you want to untie it now

Otherwise, if you talk to Freja, go to 240

If you talk to Sai, go to 270

If you return to the elevator gargoyle, go to 519

519

You turn from Sai, Fairy and Freja back to the only path on, the lift up to Lyric. Only Fairy acknowledges your departure with a small wave as you and Kyla ascend to the abuse suite.

Go to 347

520

Clawed Dragon swoops!

Clawed Dragon spews a ball of fire at you.

You are engulfed in a blaze.

The **purple glow** implodes in thick yellow gas. You can no longer use the **purple glow**.

You collapse, exhausted.

Clawed Dragon soars up and out of range.

Go to 432

521

Kyla raises the **purple stick** and casts a 'DEEP INFERNO' spell on Duke Elf, Mysterious Elf, Clawed Dragon and Lyric.

Smash! An outstanding hit.

Duke Elf is bleeding.

Smash! An outstanding hit.

Mysterious Elf collapses, exhausted.

Mysterious Elf drops **8 glittered pebbles**.

If you want to keep them, note you have gained **8 glittered pebbles**.

Clawed Dragon is out of range.

Clawed Dragon is unaffected.

Lyric is out of range.

Lyric is unaffected.

Duke Elf beats his chest and hollers for help.

Massive Elf comes to his aid!

Massive Elf attacks Sai.

Sai giggles and skips out of range.

Sai is unaffected.

Sai moves next.

If you want Sai to attack Massive Elf, go to 202

If you want Sai to attack Duke Elf, go to 412

522

You cross your fingers and hope for the best.

Go to 293

523

Clawed Dragon swoops!

Clawed Dragon spews a ball of fire at you.

Clawed Dragon misses!

You are unaffected.

Lyric leaps down from Clawed Dragon's back.

Go to 159

524

You attack Hob Goblin.

Hob Goblin successfully defends himself with the **blue shield**.

Hob Goblin is unaffected.

Hob Goblin raises the **purple stick** and casts a 'DEEP BOLT' spell on you.

Bang! A stunning hit.

The **blue shield** cracks and snaps in two. You can no longer use the **blue shield**.

You are bleeding.

You move next.

Go to 434

525

You enter a small, square room with pale blue brick walls. In each wall is a single door. Above, the ceiling is lined with hundreds of long, sharp spears, like a massive jury of guilty fingers pointing down at you. You take another step into the room. A quiet, mechanical whirring sound catches your ear.

"The ceiling!" shouts Kyla.

You follow her line of sight. The entire spiked ceiling has started to lower and its deadly spears are gradually closing down on you. It is falling too fast to reach any of the other doors!

If you leave by the door through which you came, go to 53

If you hold up your arms to push against the spiked ceiling, go to 485

526

Cobra shield flickers.

Nothing happens.

Smash! An outsatnding hit.

Cobra shield implodes in thick yellow gas. You can no longer use **cobra shield**.

You are bleeding.
Go to 142

527

Kyla raises the **purple stick** and casts a '**DEEP PORTAL**' spell on you and her.

Everything starts to blur.

"Kyla?"

Nothing.

"Kyla! Are you all right?"

The rain beats harder than ever against the window of Kyla's flat. Kyla's slumped on the floor, her head resting on the low table between Adrienne's extinguished candles. As you gently shake her shoulder she wakes with a start. She looks round wildly, as if she has never seen her own flat before.

"No! Lyric?"

"It's OK," you reassure her, holding her quivering body close to your chest. "We're safe."

Everything is as you left it. The settee, littered with papers, the results of Adrienne and you trying to guess the lyrics to 'Love Shack', what feels like a hundred lifetimes ago. The same mounds of clothes and stuffed toys all about the floor. Three cold mugs of tea on top of the telly.

"Adrienne..." Kyla pushes herself free of your embrace. "We... left her, didn't we? I remember. Lyric's forces. They were so strong... We gave up. Oh my God. What have we done?"

A clap of thunder outside makes you both jump. You stand up again, not sure what to say.

"We did all we could," you try. "It was so crazy there. Doesn't even seem real..."

"But it was real," asserts Kyla. "Or else where is Adrienne now? Stranded in another world, at that elf monster's mercy. What have we done? She wouldn't have abandoned us. Never.

What are we going to say to everyone? Her family? How will we tell them that she's... she's gone?"

You cannot answer. You stand a moment in silence, then, slowly, you collect the mugs of tea, take them out into the kitchen. Behind you, you can hear Kyla start to cry. You know you should go back through and comfort her. You know what you should do.

Standing over the sink, you slowly pour away the cold tea, watching it drain down the plug hole as the rain builds outside.

You turn on the hot tap and begin to scrub the mugs clean.